The Two-Witness Rule

The Two-Witness Rule

A Novel

BY

WILLIAM ELEAZER

Elex Publishers, Inc.
St. Petersburg, Florida

This is a book of fiction. Names, characters, and incidents are products of the author's imagination or are used fictitiously. Any resemblance to actual events or persons, living or dead, is entirely coincidental. Real places are occasionally used to give a sense of reality, but all events involving such places are fictional.

ISBN-10: 0982474717
ISBN (Print): 9780982474716

ISBN (eBook): 9780982474723

Library of Congress Control Number: 2015937097
Elex Publishers, Incorporated, Saint Petersburg, Florida

Published by
Elex Publishers, Inc.
5 Crescent Place South
St. Petersburg, Florida 33711
Contact publishers at www.elexpublishers.com or call (800)-546-ELEX (3539)

Background cover photo of Forsyth Park Fountain by Gary Mazzie. Used by permission.
For other work by Gary Mazzie, see www.garystravels.com

Printed by CreateSpace, An Amazon.com Company

Printed in the United States of America

First Edition

Dedication

As with my first two novels, *Savannah Law* and *The Indictments*, ***The Two-Witness Rule*** is dedicated to the citizens of Savannah, Georgia, the beautiful city that has inspired so many artists and writers.

Other Novels by William Eleazer

***Savannah Law*, 2010 Gold Medal Winner for Adult Fiction, awarded by the Florida Publishers Association.** A young professor's obsession with a female student at Savannah College of Law takes a surprising turn after Max Gordon, one of the nation's most successful criminal defense attorneys, arrives in Savannah for a high profile trial. Its aftermath leaves the lives of all involved changed forever. This is a novel about the law, jury trials, lawyers, law schools, and law students. If you love Savannah, the city, you will love *Savannah Law*, the novel.

***The Indictments*, © 2012.** A brazen robbery by a masked man at one of Savannah's finest restaurants results in the murder of a teenage girl and murder indictments against two defendants. *The Indictments* is a sequel to *Savannah Law* and brings back Scott Marino, the young assistant DA, to once more face ace defense attorney Max Gordon in a Chatham County courtroom. With beautiful Savannah as the locale, this legal thriller will give you many hours of enjoyable and exciting reading. The colorful characters and realistic courtroom drama in *The Indictments* will keep you riveted on the twisting plot until the unforgettable final chapter, making it a perfect read for the beach or while sitting by the fire on a cold winter day!

The Two-Witness Rule

On the trial of a defendant charged with perjury, the judge should instruct the jury on the two-witness rule. *Potts v. State*, 8 Ga. App. 799 (1949)

Chapter One

Thursday, June 5, 2008

Attorney Max Gordon stood a few feet in front of the judge's bench in Courtroom K of the Chatham County Courthouse. He was in familiar surroundings. Although he was from Chicago, he had served as defense counsel in three felony trials in this same courtroom.

A short, rotund man, Gordon had a sharp pointed nose and thinning hair, parted in the middle and held in place by a thick layer of hair spray. His diminutive size and appearance was quite deceptive, as he was one of the nation's best known and most successful criminal defense attorneys. His reputation—combined with the fact that his client in those three previous trials was John Harrison, son of David Harrison, a former Georgia senator and then-candidate for governor—created media frenzy during each trial. All of the trials were televised live throughout the state and served as a front-page news story in all Georgia newspapers.

"Maxwell E. Gordon, how do you plead?"

Max Gordon had heard a similar question asked hundreds of times in his career as a defense attorney, but this was the first time the question was preceded by *his* name. But there he was, standing stooped with a colorless and tightened face, looking down at the carpet in front of the judge's bench. He lifted his head as Judge Vesely finished the question. Before he could answer, his attorney answered for him.

"The defendant pleads not guilty, Your Honor. We waive formal reading of the indictment but request a copy and a list of witnesses. We are going to opt in on discovery and we request trial by jury. We ask for ten days to file motions."

Gordon's attorney, Charles Samarkos, was one of Savannah's most experienced and respected criminal defense attorneys. Gordon had hired him immediately after being arrested on charges of subornation of perjury and influencing witnesses. The indictments alleged that Gordon paid two eyewitnesses to testify falsely at Harrison's second trial. That second trial was a retrial for a robbery conviction that had been overturned by the Georgia Court of Appeals. The acquittal meant that Harrison was free, after serving almost a year in prison. But his freedom was short lived. He was arrested within days after his acquittal, this time for felony murder of a teenage girl during the commission of another robbery. Once again Gordon traveled to Savannah to defend him, but this time Gordon was unsuccessful, and his client was convicted.

Scott Marino, the young assistant DA who had assisted in prosecuting all three of the Harrison trials and who was now assigned to this case, stood at the prosecution table. He spoke immediately after Samarkos.

"Your Honor, I would like to be heard now on a matter concerning the bail arrangements for Mr. Gordon."

Samarkos and Gordon turned quickly toward the young prosecutor, both with puzzled looks on their faces. Samarkos spoke before Scott could continue.

"Your Honor, that was settled by Judge Feather at a bond hearing the morning after his arrest. There is nothing to be heard. At the bond hearing, the state argued for a $100,000 bail bond and we argued for his release on his personal recognizance. Mr. Gordon is one of the most respected attorneys in the entire country. There is zero chance he would not show to fight these outrageous charges. The request for a monetary bond in this case was—and remains—a preposterous overreach by the district attorney. While almost any monetary bond could be easily met by Mr. Gordon, we vigorously fought monetary bail because it was a professional insult rather than a measure to ensure Mr. Gordon's presence for trial. Judge Feather set a $10,000 bond. We disagree with it, but we accept it. Now apparently the DA's office is not satisfied with this amount. So be it. They had their chance. There is no matter to discuss."

Scott looked up at Judge Vesely, awaiting her response. The judge said nothing, but extended an open hand toward Scott, indicating permission for him to respond.

"Your Honor," Scott said, "I am not proposing any change in the bail amount. As Mr. Samarkos correctly states, Judge Feather has settled that. But what we are not satisfied with is this attorney, who is under an indictment for these serious felonies, continuing to appear in court representing defendants in numerous cases in various jurisdictions across the country."

Scott turned and faced Gordon before continuing. "These are very grave crimes. Mr. Gordon is charged not only with being aware that perjury was to be committed, but he was the monetary force behind it. These crimes are classic *crimen falsi* crimes, the embodiment of dishonesty and corruption."

His voice was sharp as he continued, his eyes fixed sternly on Max Gordon. "Perjured testimony strikes at the very core of the criminal justice system."

He paused briefly, then turned to face Judge Vesely. "But more than that, Your Honor, by securing the acquittal of John Harrison by perjured testimony, he put the defendant on the street where he was able to secure a weapon, commit a robbery, and kill an innocent teenager during that robbery. Angela Voss, a young high school senior, out with her family celebrating the news of her scholarship to Emory—murdered by John Harrison. She would still be alive except for Max Gordon's criminal acts, as outlined in this indictment. Conviction on the two counts of subornation of perjury carries a possible sentence of twenty years confinement with at least two years mandatory. This man should be precluded from setting foot in *any* courthouse as a defense attorney until he answers these charges in *this* courthouse as a defendant."

As Max Gordon's face reddened, his eyebrows squeezed together into a sharp crease. He lowered his head, clenched his jaw, and his tightened eyes looked directly at the floor. This was a new situation for Gordon. Here he was in his favorite environment, a courtroom, and all he could do was repeatedly open and close his fingers in a tight fist. He bit his lip but remained silent, as he knew he must.

"Mr. Samarkos, do you wish to respond?" asked Judge Vesely.

"Of course, Your Honor. And may I emphasize that I am appalled at such an unlawful and outrageous request being made by this assistant district attorney. Mr. Marino seems to misconstrue an accusation with conviction. He presents no authority for this court to impose such restrictions as part of bail. Mr. Gordon is licensed to practice law in Illinois, New York, and Ohio, and only those states can impose such restrictions on his practice. Such action as requested by Mr. Marino is without precedence, and I trust Your Honor will quickly deny it."

Judge Vesely looked toward Scott. "Mr. Marino, did you argue for this additional sanction at the initial bail hearing?"

"No, Your Honor. And I regret that I did not."

"No need for regret, Mr. Marino, as I'm sure it would have been denied, just as I'm going to do. There will be no such restriction added. But I caution Mr. Gordon to follow the rules of each state in which he is licensed. Some states require that upon being arrested, the attorney notify the state bar or some governmental agency. That is the attorney's responsibility, not mine. Now, for a date for hearing motions. I'm here only for this arraignment. This is Judge McCabe's case. He is in trials this week and next week, but he informed me he wants to hear motions in this case on June 26. Is that satisfactory with counsel?"

Scott quickly checked his cell phone where he maintained a copy of his calendar. He was the first to respond. "Yes, Your Honor, that's satisfactory with the prosecution."

The defendant and his counsel were quickly involved in a hushed but animated discussion. Samarkos turned to the judge and said, "Your Honor, may I have a few moments to confer with my client?"

"Yes, take a moment, Mr. Samarkos."

Samarkos and Gordon turned and moved a few steps backward and continued their quiet conversation. Scott could not hear them, but there was obviously a conflict with the date. Scott sat down at the prosecutor's table and waited. Finally Samarkos turned and faced the judge.

"Your Honor, I am available for the hearing on June 26, but Mr. Gordon is scheduled for a federal criminal trial in Cleveland that week, a trial which is expected to last three weeks."

Judge Vesely pushed her body back forcefully into her chair, and her face made a stern expression. Scott quickly rose and said, "May I be heard, Your Honor?"

But before Judge Vesely could reply, he continued. "This is exactly why I asked that this defendant's bail be modified to preclude him from setting foot in *any* courthouse until he answers these charges in *this* courthouse. I submit, that as a condition of continuing his bail, he should be prohibited from appearing as an attorney in any court in any jurisdiction, federal or state."

Samarkos turned quickly toward the judge. "Your Honor, this is outrageous. We have already—"

Judge Vesely cut him off before he could continue. "Counsel," she said, leaning forward and in a loud and obviously annoyed voice. "Enough! This is a serious issue! And counsel—all of you—be seated."

She paused, and in a calmer voice, continued. "Frankly this is the first case I've had in which the defendant is a defense attorney and actively trying cases in various jurisdictions. In fact, as far as I can recall, this is the first time I've had any case involving an attorney as an accused. We've had our share in Savannah, but fortunately they haven't landed on my docket." Then she sat back in her chair, resting her elbows on its arms, and folding her hands across her lap. She looked across the courtroom at a far wall, her face appearing to be in deep thought. The courtroom stilled.

"Perhaps I should revisit my decision on bail conditions," she said quietly, almost to herself.

Samarkos was once again on his feet. "Your Honor, I believe I have a solution, if I may be heard."

"Of course, Mr. Samarkos. Let's see how your solution compares to the one I'm about to announce."

"After conferring with Mr. Gordon, Your Honor, it appears there is no conflict after all. He has agreed to waive his personal appearance at all pretrial hearings. He is satisfied with my representing him in his absence on June 26 and all future pretrial hearings, and we will present that in writing. His bail conditions will thus need no modification."

"Then that should settle any conflict. Do you agree, Mr. Marino?"

Scott stood and faced the judge. There was a look of displeasure on his face as he spoke. "Your Honor, I do not agree. This defendant should be appearing at all pretrial hearings. He's out on bail, and requiring his appearance at pretrial hearings is one way to assure he's around for trial. Additionally, he needs to be present so that he understands the status of the case should there be plea discussions. If he's not here, observing what is taking place at these pretrial hearings, how can he make an informed decision should there be a plea offer? This defendant is facing serious felony charges—charges of instigating perjury, Your Honor, *perjury*—in an armed robbery trial. He should not be out and about in the country serving as defense counsel in any trial, anywhere."

As Scott spoke, Max Gordon's face and neck once again reddened. His neck veins expanded and his lips tightened. He placed his right hand on the side of his neck and patted it rapidly with his fingers. His breathing was short and rapid. Samarkos glanced at him with concern and was about to stand and object to Scott's comments when Judge Vesely interrupted.

"Mr. Marino, I have ruled on the bail conditions. And it is customary for a party to waive his or her right to appear in person at any pretrial hearings. Mr. Samarkos, since you have offered to place that waiver in the record in written form, we will leave it at that. Judge McCabe will hear any motions counsel may have at nine a.m. on June 26. Now, anything else from counsel?"

Neither counsel had anything further. Judge Vesely called the next case on the morning's docket, and Scott picked up his file and prepared to leave the courtroom. As he passed the defense table, he heard Max Gordon say to Samarkos in a loud whisper, "Get that arrogant son-of-a-bitch off this case!"

Scott turned to face Gordon and smiled. Gordon clenched both fists and took a step toward Scott. Samarkos quickly extended his left arm over Gordon's chest. Scott turned and headed for the exit.

As Scott left the courtroom, Samarkos picked up his briefcase and led Gordon out into the corridor. Gordon's face was still crimson. They walked to the end of the corridor where there was a window overlooking the street below. It was midmorning and the street was flush with traffic. A light rain had just stopped, and the sidewalks were alive with men and women hurrying in both directions, some holding umbrellas over their heads and others stepping left and right to avoid them. They stood silently, peering out the window for a long while. Samarkos was the first to speak.

"Max, I would like to meet with you tomorrow morning. We have a lot to cover. Can you be at my office at nine?" Samarkos deliberately avoided mentioning the confrontation with Scott.

However, the young prosecutor was *all* that was on Gordon's mind. His thoughts flashed back to May 1, in this same courthouse where he was defending John Harrison for murder. As the jury returned a verdict of guilty, TV cameras were trained on the defense table, where Gordon and the defendant stood. Gordon had seen that scene only once in a TV clip after the trial, but it had played hundreds of times in his mind. He had watched as the judge polled the jury and set a sentencing date. As soon as the judge announced that the court was adjourned, while Gordon was still standing and stunned from the verdict, he felt a hand on his shoulder. He turned and faced a man he had never met. "Mr. Gordon," the man said, "I'm Carl DeBickero, an agent for the Georgia Bureau of Investigation. I have a warrant for your arrest for subornation of perjury. Sir, place your hands behind your back. *Now!*"

Those words kept echoing through Gordon's head. And he recalled that as the agent said "Now," he saw Scott Marino from the corner of his eye. He wasn't smiling, but he had a look of pure satisfaction on his face. And now, this day, in that same courthouse, he not only had to enter his plea to that charge, but he had to listen to that same young prosecutor argue that Gordon "should not be out and about in the country serving as defense counsel in any trial, anywhere." *This was beyond unbearable!*

"I'll be there in the morning," Gordon said. "And the first thing I want to discuss is how you plan to get that little prick off this case. You may not be able to get the charges dismissed, but you can get that young punk dismissed. I don't want to see his smug-ass face again in any courtroom. That's your first order of business."

"Max, I can understand your anger, but it's misdirected. You wouldn't benefit by having someone else prosecute this case. Marino is the least experienced prosecutor in the DA's office—less than two years and some of that as a clinic student. Forget it. We have some important matters to discuss tomorrow."

"Maybe you didn't hear me. Let me know if you have a hearing problem. I said I want that shithead off the case. I probably can't buy him, he suffers from some sort of ethics disease. You recall what I told you when I hired you—that money is no problem? Spend what you need to spend. Now, look at my lips. I'm about to say something you need to hear. I want Marino off this case. Now, did you hear me?"

Samarkos immediately stood erect, squared his shoulders, and looked directly into Gordon's eyes. He held the gaze for a long moment.

"I have your message, Max, but I'm your attorney, not your lackey. I'll look into everything that I know—or you can provide—that may be grounds for Marino being removed, and I'll file any motion that's appropriate. Perhaps there's a conflict of interest. I'll look into it, but so far, I don't see it."

"Well, look harder. I want him *off*."

"You've made that clear. Frankly, I'm surprised the DA has assigned this junior assistant to this case. My advice is to let it go. You think about it. You don't want to replace the least experienced attorney with the most experienced. And that's what you'll get if Marino goes."

"Listen, Charles. I'm paying you six hundred an hour because you're supposed to be the smartest lawyer in town, and if you're that smart, it shouldn't be a big problem. This trial is going to last a week, maybe two. But I don't want to watch that little prick strutting around the jury like he's a big dick. Not two weeks, not one week, *not one fucking day*. He's gotta go. Have I made that clear?"

"You've made it clear that you want him off the case. You haven't made it clear that there is anything we can do *legally* to accomplish that, or that it's good trial strategy for it to occur. We'll discuss it in the morning."

Samarkos picked up his briefcase and walked rapidly down the corridor. He did not look back. He mused to himself that this was going to be an exceedingly difficult case, made more difficult by an exceedingly difficult client.

After leaving the courtroom, Scott didn't get ten steps down the corridor before hearing a familiar voice behind him. "Hey, Scott, got a minute?"

Scott turned to see Bill Baldwin, a reporter for the *South Georgia Times*. Bill had covered the two armed robbery trials of John Harrison as well as his murder trial that had ended just five weeks earlier. Scott and Bill had established a professional friendship that had served both of them quite well. In fact, it was a tip from Bill that had led to the investigation that ended with the murder indictment against Harrison. And as information became available about how the investigation was preceding, Scott made sure that Bill and his newspaper were the first to know. He was aware of the internal guidelines about releasing information. He didn't know if he had broken them, but he knew they were often seriously *bent*.

"Bill, you know I always try to make time for you, but I've really got some pressing matters upstairs that need attention. Can't talk now." Scott turned and continued down the corridor to the elevator. Bill was right behind him.

"How about lunch at Churchill's? You gotta eat somewhere."

Churchill's Bar and Grill, about eight blocks away on West Bay, was a pub where the two met occasionally. Bill was a regular there.

"Can't do," said Scott. "My day is filled."

"Then after work. Churchill's. I'll buy."

"Sorry, Bill, I'm meeting Jennifer at six at the Library."

Jennifer, Scott's long-time girlfriend, would be entering her senior year in the fall at Savannah College of Law—generally known as "Savannah Law." Scott and Jennifer met when Scott was a senior and she an entering first-year student. As president of the Student Bar Association, Scott was assisting with student orientation, which Jennifer was attending. He invited her out the first day they met, and they had been a couple ever since. Now, almost two years later, they were very much in love and looking forward to their life together. Jennifer was not enrolled in any law classes for the summer, but was on campus almost daily, conducting research for her Advanced Research Project, the "ARP," a comprehensive research project required of all Savannah Law students before their final semester. It was a major undertaking.

Bill and Scott had now reached the bank of courthouse elevators. A door to an elevator opened, and Scott quickly walked in. As the doors closed, Scott heard Bill shout, "I'll call you."

And Scott knew he would. In fact, the phone was ringing in Scott's office as soon as he sat down at his desk. Scott picked up and answered.

"Hello, Bill."

"Scott, I really would like to have a chat. Won't take long. How about meeting you at the Library about five thirty? When Jennifer arrives I'll pay the tab and leave quickly—that's a promise."

That sounded reasonable to Scott. He wasn't trying to avoid Bill, but he was in fact quite busy that day. He enjoyed their conversations, and frequently Bill provided information on people and events in the community that Scott found important to his job. Bill had been covering the Chatham County Courthouse for over twenty years and had a wealth of knowledge about judges, detectives, police officers, and administrative personnel. He had been a solid confidant during the Harrison murder trial.

"OK, five thirty."

Chapter Two

Thursday, June 5

The "Library" was really the Library Bar and Grill, located within a block of Savannah Law. Scott had been a frequent customer during his three years as a student and had become good friends with the owner, Jaak Terras, and Jaak's brother Juri, who served as the assistant manager and head bartender. The building got its name from its original purpose, a Chatham County public library built in the 1920s. The granite-faced building was solidly built, with heart-of-pine floors and twenty-foot ceilings for summer comfort before air conditioning. It had been abandoned for years after a more modern library was built nearby. Jaak purchased the deteriorating building directly from the county and, after almost a year of renovations, opened the Library Bar and Grill the same year Savannah College of Law opened as a new law school. Scott loved the place and went there often with Jennifer.

Scott arrived a little early for the 5:30 meeting with Bill. As he walked through the large oak double-doors of the entryway, he saw Juri behind the bar, polishing wine glasses. As soon as Juri spotted Scott, he began shaking his head slowly from side to side, with a sad look on his face. Scott had expected it. Juri and Scott were avid

Atlanta Braves fans, and Scott had read in the morning paper that the Braves lost to the Marlins the night before, 4-6.

"Can't even beat a lousy Marlins team," Juri said, as Scott took a seat at the bar. "We got *six* guys making over a million this year, and none of them can find home plate. We didn't make the playoffs last year, and if they don't get their act together soon, we won't make it this year. You think Bobby Cox can manage this team to the playoffs?"

As he was talking, Juri poured Scott a draft in an iced mug and slid it eight feet down the bar top, stopping directly in front of Scott. It was a technique Juri perfected during the twelve years he had presided at the bar. And as always, he followed up with a pumped fist.

"Sure, Juri, we'll make the playoffs. It's early. We're over five hundred now, and most of the season is still ahead. You worry too much."

"That's what I do best, worry. Takes my mind off things. You meeting Jennifer here tonight?"

"Yes, and Bill Baldwin in a few minutes." Juri knew Baldwin; he was a frequent customer.

"Good. I've got something special on tap from a brewery in Asheville I want him to taste. He always asks if I have anything new." Just then, Juri saw Bill in the entryway. "There he comes now."

"Hi, Juri. Hi, Scott," Bill said as he took a seat at the bar next to Scott. Many of the tables in the grill were occupied, but Bill and Scott were the only two sitting at the bar.

"Juri, got anything new on tap?" asked Bill. Juri gave a knowing smile and a wink to Scott and went to get a frosty mug. He filled the mug with the new Asheville brew and a perfect head, and slid it down the bar top.

"I wish just one of the Brave's pitchers was as accurate, just one," Juri said. He pumped his fist in celebration as the mug came to a slow stop in front of Bill. "Which reminds me of a new joke. This one's a reporter joke—for Bill. Want to hear it?"

He didn't wait for a response; he never did. He had an unlimited reservoir of jokes, and he was an unceasing joke teller—and he was good at it. Even a joke that bombed ended being quite funny when told by Juri.

"This guy—he's a tourist, taking pictures in Forsyth Park—sees a big dog attacking a young boy. Dog's jaws around the boy's neck. The guy rushes over, tackles the dog, pulls him off the boy and kills the dog—strangles him with his bare hands. News reporter sees it happen, congratulates the man and tells him the headline the next day is gonna read, '*Valiant Local Man Saves Child by Killing Vicious Animal.*' Guy says he's not from Savannah. Reporter says, 'Well then, the headline will read, "*Georgia Man Saves Child by Killing Wild Dog.*"' Man says, 'Actually, I'm from Connecticut.' Reporter says, 'Well then, let me think . . . Why sure, the headline is gonna read, "*Yankee Kills Family Pet*"'!"

And with that, Juri began to smile, then let out a loud laugh, joined in by Bill and Scott, but the one who enjoyed it the most, as always, was Juri.

"Juri, that wasn't as bad as your usual lawyer jokes," said Scott. "And before you begin another one, Bill and I have some business." Scott picked up his beer and motioned Bill to follow him to a quiet corner at the end of the bar.

When they were settled, Scott said, "So you want me to write your story for tomorrow's paper? Must be a slow news day when the star reporter for the *South Georgia Times* hangs out on a hard bench in a courtroom listening to arraignments."

"Not just any arraignment, Scott. Max Gordon's arraignment. You may not have noticed, but there were several other reporters there, including Roger Curlin, who covered all the Harrison trials for the *National Law Journal*. Max Gordon on trial is not a slow news day. And, no, I don't want any lawyer writing my story—I respect my readers too much to subject them to that. But I do have a couple questions, and the first one is about that motion to yank Gordon's law license."

"It wasn't a motion to yank the license, just a motion to keep a lawyer who's indicted for serious felonies—funding perjured testimony and tampering with witnesses—from continuing to appear in court as a defense counsel. You got a problem with that?"

"Looks like the judge did. What did the DA—and Joe Fasi—have to say? Isn't Fasi still the felony chief?"

"He is." Scott paused a moment, making eye contact before continuing. "Now, Bill, we're off the record, right? None of this gets into your story."

"You know that's the agreement with all our conversations. And no change unless we both say otherwise," replied Bill.

"Good. Really, Bill, I hadn't planned to make that motion. But it had been bothering me for days, just thinking about that slimeball flying around the country appearing in court almost daily, while under indictment. So, as I looked on and listened as Samarkos entered Gordon's 'not guilty' pleas, it really burned me. He's guilty of more than just those felonies—he's really responsible for the death of the teenager that John Harrison murdered. I thought of Daniel Voss and his wife going out to celebrate the good news of their daughter's scholarship. How can your only child get murdered by just going out to a nice restaurant in Savannah with her family? It didn't have to happen. Without that perjured testimony, John Harrison would still be in jail and Angela Voss would be entering Emory on her way to a medical degree instead of lying in a grave in Greenwich Cemetery. Sure, I should have at least run the motion by Fasi to get his take on it, but it was a last minute decision."

"I understand, Scott. I will be filing a story on Gordon's arraignment for tomorrow's paper. You want me to leave your motion out of the article?"

"I have no objection, Bill, and even if I did, it's a public record now. Print whatever you want to print."

"I think the public will be interested, so I'll probably include it. New question: You charged him with two counts of subornation of perjury plus two counts of influencing witnesses. Why both crimes?"

"Well, to prove the subornation charge, we have to prove that the witness actually lied under oath. But to prove a charge of influencing witnesses, we only have to prove he offered a benefit or reward to the witness to commit perjury—in this case $250,000 each. Doesn't matter if they did or did not actually lie. The penalty is much less—five years for each charge. But if we prove they actually committed perjury, the penalty is a max of ten years for each charge and a minimum of one."

"How's the case shaping up? You say he's slimy; is he slick enough to beat this charge?"

"No question he's slick," Scott replied. "But we have a strong case. You remember his sidekick, Clarence Wilborn—the attorney who sponsored him for the retrial?"

"Sure," said Bill. "Weasel looking fellow, from Macon. I recall he was indicted along with Gordon."

"Right," said Scott. "And he's given a complete confession. Gordon negotiated the perjury terms with the two witnesses, and Wilborn was the delivery guy—personally delivered $250,000 in cash to each of 'em."

Bill looked surprised at this. "Why would he confess? He's a lawyer—seems he would know enough to shut his mouth and keep it shut."

"He was also a part-time drug dealer, a two-bit player in a major syndicate—one of the biggest illegal drug operations in the Southeast. His law practice was in Macon, but his drug involvement was in both Macon and Atlanta. When he was arrested by the feds, the GBI was notified. Carl DeBickero, the GBI agent in charge of the perjury investigation, went to Atlanta and negotiated a deal with the feds to let Georgia handle the case. There were enough big fish from the syndicate for the feds to fry, so they didn't mind turning a little fish over to the state. Fulton County now has the case. Wilborn had been defending drug cases for several years—that's how he got involved with the syndicate. He quickly realized there was enough evidence to put him away for life if the authorities wanted to. And he believed they wanted to. So he cut a deal with the Fulton County DA which requires that he assist DeBickero with the perjury case. Right now I'm not sure of all of the specifics in the Fulton County case, but if he cooperates in the investigation and testifies against Gordon, it's a pretty favorable plea deal—max of ten years or even less, depending on how well he cooperates. And they agreed to let him out on bail until Gordon's trial. So, that's how we got the case. I wasn't even aware of Wilborn's arrest until after Gordon was arrested."

"You say he delivered $250,000 to each of the lying witnesses? Half a million total? That's a lot of bills. And whose account did it come from—Senator Harrison's?"

"Of course the senator funded it, so to speak. At least he was the source of the funds, but they were part of Gordon's legal fees. Gordon could demand any fee he wanted. Senator Harrison was in a tough campaign, and his son sitting in prison was not helpful. Only thing on the senator's mind back then was to get his son out of prison, and he believed Gordon was the man who could do it. Remember, Harrison is one of the richest men in Georgia—worth over a hundred million according to several news accounts. Whether he knew some of the exorbitant fees were going for witness payoffs, we don't know and probably will never know. He had a series of strokes last winter and is reported to be both mentally and physically incapacitated."

Bill interrupted. "But how did Wilborn get his hands on that much cash? Banks don't just dole out that kind of money without a lot of paper work. Even as little as $10,000 requires a Currency Transaction Report to the feds, and that creates a paper trail that's easily traced."

"No bank," said Scott. "Remember—he had contacts in the syndicate—they deal in cash and had plenty. Wilborn introduced

Gordon to one of the higher-ups in the syndicate, and Gordon took care of the details. Probably cost him a big premium above the cash he got, but those guys know how to wash a transaction to make the deal appear clean. I don't know the details—not sure even DeBickero knows, but the deal was done and Wilborn headed out with the cash. Gordon had hired some hoodlum to contact the witnesses to make the deal, so he already had commitments from the witnesses. All Wilborn had to do was get in his vehicle and deliver. He drove to Denver to pay off Johnson, then to Savannah for Patel—alone. Took his time, careful to drive the speed limit. Didn't want to get stopped with that much cash. Three thousand miles round trip."

"I'm surprised it got delivered. There he was, alone with half a million in cash. I'm amazed that a crook like Wilborn didn't stop along the way—rent a storage shed, stash it, and disappear for a few years," Bill said.

"He probably now wishes he had," Scott said. "I also wish he had—Angela Voss would still be alive and John Harrison would be serving ten years."

"What about the witnesses—Patel and the guy from Colorado? I know Patel was arrested. But what about the other guy?"

"Josh Johnson. He was also arrested," Scott replied. "Patel's out on bail. Initially Johnson fought extradition from Colorado but finally gave up. He's being escorted back to Savannah this weekend. We're negotiating with Patel's attorney for a plea deal, and we'll do the same with Johnson when he gets here. The main culprit in this case is, of course, Gordon, and Gordon's our major target. These two witnesses were clean as far as we know until Gordon entered the case. I would like to see him put away for life, but if we can get twenty years, even ten years, I'll be satisfied."

"If they don't accept the pretrial, how strong is your case against Patel and Johnson?"

"Well, both admitted to Carl DeBickero that they received the cash. They could hardly deny it—Wilborn had taken photos of the delivery with both of them looking at a suitcase filled with $250,000 cash and smiling broadly for the camera. The photos, according to Wilborn, were taken at the direction of Max Gordon, apparently to confirm for Gordon that Wilborn actually delivered the funds. Wilborn gave the photos to DeBickero—a big bargaining chip in cutting his own pretrial deal."

"Are you lead counsel?"

"So far, but I expect Fasi will sit with me at trial, just as he did in the murder trial. But that's assuming I'm still on the case when it gets to trial. I expect that Samarkos may make a motion to have me dismissed from prosecuting the case."

Bill's face showed surprise and concern. "Why, Scott?"

"I don't think his client is happy with me," replied Scott, with a smile. "As we were leaving the courtroom this morning, Gordon said to Samarkos, just loud enough for me to hear, that he wanted that 'arrogant son-of-a-bitch off this case.' I couldn't imagine he meant me," Scott said with a chuckle. "Am I an arrogant son-of-a-bitch, Bill? I swear he was looking straight at me when he said it."

"Well, I can't speak to your ancestry, but you are a bit arrogant. Is that grounds to have you dismissed from the case?"

"Hardly. But if he wants me off the case, I'm sure Samarkos will try to find some other grounds."

"Are there any?"

"No, but that won't keep them from trying. Throw some mud balls and hope one sticks. One common ground for dismissing an attorney is for conflict of interest. But I don't have any conflict. I wasn't the investigator and wasn't a member of the grand jury. Never had any dealing with the guy except as opposing counsel in three trials. Sure, I dislike the slimy bastard, but it's OK for the prosecutor to dislike the defendant. If that were grounds for dismissal they wouldn't be able to find a prosecutor anywhere south of Chattanooga to try this case. I'm sworn to give him a fair trial, not enjoy his company. Nothing that—"

Scott did not finish his sentence. He looked to the center of the long bar. There was Jennifer, talking with Juri. Scott smiled as he watched. She was radiantly beautiful, and as always, she brought a smile to his face. Bill turned in the same direction.

"I see Jennifer's here, and I recall my promise to pay the tab and leave quickly," Bill said, as he reached for his billfold.

"No. Come on over and say 'hi,'" Scott said.

Scott and Bill moved from the privacy of the bar alcove to the center of the bar where Jennifer was sitting. A tonic and lime was on the bar in front of her.

Scott gave her a quick kiss on her cheek, and said, "We didn't see you come in, but I see you've been here long enough to get served. Sorry." He took a seat next to Jennifer.

"I saw that you and Bill were deep in conversation—didn't want to interrupt." Jennifer turned to face Bill. "Hi, Bill," she said. "Haven't seen you in a while."

"Yes, my bad luck, but nice to see you again. I stole a little time from Scott, but I'm leaving now so you two can catch up." Bill placed some cash on the counter. As he was turning to leave, Juri stepped over to face them.

"Can't leave yet, Bill. I've got a story for Jennifer." Juri was already beginning to smile, and Scott was trying to suppress a smile. He knew what would follow—Juri's "story" would be a blonde joke. Bill slid into a bar stool and placed an elbow on the bar to listen.

"Three blondes were walking through a forest when they came upon a set of tracks. First blonde says, 'Those are deer tracks.' The second blonde says, 'No, those are elk tracks.' Third blonde says, 'You're both wrong, those are moose tracks.' And they were still arguing when the train hit them!"

And with that, Juri's smile turned into a broad grin. Then, the grin turned into a burst of laughter as he shifted his eyes from one to the other, looking for approval. Juri's laughter was catching, and as usual, his audience followed. It was always the same, the good jokes as well as the bad.

"Juri, you've already told one reporter joke," Bill said. "I'm leaving before you think of another. And thanks, Scott, for the update on Gordon. Hope to see you again soon—and, of course, you too, Jennifer." Bill headed for the exit.

At that moment, a loud crash of dishes hitting the floor resounded throughout the building. It came from the restaurant area and was followed by loud but indistinct voices.

"Sounds like they need some help," Juri said, as he rushed out from behind the bar on his way to the accident.

"I think that'll keep Juri occupied a while," Scott said to Jennifer. "Saved us from having to listen to that bad lawyer joke I know he was planning." He reached for Jennifer's hand. "Come on, I found a new Italian restaurant near Forsyth Park that I want to try."

Chapter Three

Tuesday, June 17

Joe Fasi arrived at the Chatham County DA's office at 7:00 a.m., as he frequently did. He was usually the first one there. Not today. He looked down a corridor and saw a light that seemed to be coming from Scott Marino's office. He had not spoken to Scott in a few days and decided to check in.

"Good morning, Scott. Busy day today?"

"Morning, Joe. Yes, starting that Sumter Street arson case this morning. Gonna be a battle of experts. Just checking a few last minute details and the reports of my two experts. I've read about everything I can get my hands on about arson investigations—there's a ton of information out there on the Internet. But a couple of days ago I came across an article by John Lentini—he's a nationally known fire investigator, forty years experience. He claims that much of the information taught to arson investigators is mythical."

"Myths that impact your case?"

"Maybe. For example, my experts give as one reason they believe an accelerant was used was the speed of the fire, and that the angle of the V-pattern indicates the speed. Lentini says that a rapidly burning fire doesn't necessarily indicate accelerants were used, and you can't tell speed from the V-pattern. Myths, he calls it. Of course, we have a lot more. I'm not relying solely on experts, but I do see a problem with some of their evidence."

"Where did you get your experts?" asked Fasi.

"Both are with the GBI."

"Well, as you say, Scott, this is a battle of experts. Let them fight it out. I'm sure your experts can handle it. You do your job and let them do theirs."

Scott was seated behind his desk. Fasi had been standing since entering but now took a seat close to Scott.

"Don't believe I've spoken to you recently about our old friend Max Gordon—anything new since his arraignment?" asked Fasi.

"Yes, got a motion yesterday from Samarkos to have me dismissed from the case. I read it but haven't worked on a response yet. I'll do that this weekend. Right now this arson trial is consuming me."

"Let me read it," said Fasi. Scott searched under a pile of papers, found the motion and handed it to Fasi.

After reading, Fasi said, "Scott, Samarkos seems to be relying mostly on the Prosecution Standards of the National District Attorneys Association. Any validity to the charges he makes?"

"Nope."

"Any reason at all that you can think of that could support your dismissal?"

"Nope."

"Then I'll prepare the response. When is the hearing?"

"Thursday, June 26. Judge McCabe has the case. But I can do it—had planned to work on it as soon as this arson trial is over, probably Friday."

"I think you have enough on your plate now—maybe too much. I'll do it. Besides, it's a complaint against you personally. It's appropriate to have someone else respond."

"Well, thanks," Scott said. In fact, he was genuinely relieved. He did have a lot on his plate.

"Have you ever had a case with Judge McCabe?" Fasi asked.

"No, this will be my first."

"He's a former prosecutor," Fasi said. "Good judge—runs a tight ship. Make me a copy of the motion. I'll prepare the response in the next day or so and send you a copy."

Fasi took a long look at Scott as he got up to leave. Scott looked tired and appeared to have lost weight. Fasi was concerned. Scott was the least experienced assistant in the felony division and was carrying a full load of felony cases. The Max Gordon case was going to require extensive work. Fasi made a mental note to try to lighten Scott's case load.

Later that morning, Fasi phoned Louise Petren, office personnel manager. "Louise, could you please look up the vacation status of Scott Marino. How many vacation days has he taken in the past year?"

"I don't have to look it up, Mr. Fasi. I know he hasn't taken a single day of vacation time since he was hired."

It did not surprise Fasi. But it concerned him. Trials are extremely exhausting, even for experienced counsel who had learned to pace themselves. Young Type A prosecutors could burn out quickly. Fasi knew he was responsible for mentoring this young assistant in the challenges he would face in his professional development; he had not until now considered potential health challenges.

Chapter Four

Thursday, June 26

Scott and Fasi were already seated at the prosecution table when Samarkos entered. Seeing that Samarkos was alone, Scott's thoughts turned to his missing client. Scott pictured Max Gordon in Cleveland, serving as defense counsel for some ultra-rich defendant who was unaware that Max was under indictment down in Savannah, Georgia, for paying witnesses to lie. Or perhaps, that special talent was the inducement for hiring Max. In any case, Scott still firmly believed that an attorney under indictment for a serious felony should not be appearing as counsel in any court. The motion he made at arraignment to include that restriction as part of Max's bail had been reported by Bill Baldwin in the *South Georgia Times*, and Scott had discussed it with Fasi the next day. Fasi had not reproached him for it; in fact, Fasi seemed to think it was rather a reasonable motion, though he was not surprised that Judge Vesely denied it.

Scott had not told Fasi of Max's demand to Samarkos to "Get that arrogant son-of-a-bitch off this case!" He did not think it was relevant to the motion to have him removed from the case. Just because Max wanted him off was certainly not grounds for removal, and he believed it would be petty and trivial to include the comment.

Though he was having second thoughts—perhaps he should have at least informed Fasi of it—it was too late now. Fasi had already submitted his response and prepared his argument.

Judge Bernard McCabe took his seat promptly at 9:00 a.m., and with the usual pageantry exhibited in all the opening sessions of Chatham County courts—several loud and startling raps on the floor by a bailiff with a tall, banner-decorated wooden staff—the court was called to order.

Judge McCabe was an imposing figure on the bench, in his late 50s, tall and broad shouldered, with his closely trimmed dark brown hair just beginning to show a bit of gray. He served in the district attorney's office for twenty years before his appointment to the bench. What Scott had heard from Fasi and other attorneys was that McCabe was a cerebral judge who carefully weighed his decisions and was rarely, if ever, reversed. He was also known as a judge who was exceptionally courteous to all parties but always in control of the courtroom. Scott welcomed that. He knew this trial would be a hard-fought case throughout. His experience had been that the prosecution of a case is much easier with a tough, controlling judge. He had seen it first hand in the first Harrison robbery trial when Judge Desano quickly showed Max Gordon that he, and not Gordon, would remain in command.

Judge McCabe spoke briefly with the clerk, then moved quickly to the business at hand. He sat back in his chair and looked at Samarkos. "I note for the record that Mr. Gordon, the defendant in this case, is not present. I also note in the file a written waiver of appearance for this session, purportedly signed by the defendant. Did you witness this signature, Mr. Samarkos?"

"I did, Your Honor. Mr. Gordon has specifically authorized me to proceed on his behalf in his absence."

"Then we'll proceed." He turned to look at Fasi. "Mr. Fasi, I see you have an associate with you. Who will be representing the prosecution?"

Fasi stood. "Your Honor, for the proceeding today, I will be representing the prosecution, but the lead counsel for this case as it proceeds will be Assistant District Attorney Scott Marino."

Scott stood and faced the judge.

"Mr. Marino, I believe this is the first time you have appeared in one of my trials."

"That is correct, Your Honor."

"Then a special welcome, Mr. Marino. Please be seated." The judge paused, then held up some papers. "I've had an opportunity to read the brief on your motion, Mr. Samarkos, as well as the prosecution's response, but if you wish, I'll hear further argument on your motion now."

Samarkos rose from his chair and walked briskly to the lectern.

"Your Honor, I realize this is a rather unusual motion, but it is one of great importance to this trial and to Mr. Gordon. I want to emphasize some of the points made in my brief. The district attorney has assigned an assistant district attorney to this case—Scott Marino—who we believe is not qualified to proceed with the prosecution. It is our position that he should be prohibited from serving as prosecutor of the charges against Mr. Gordon. Two years ago, Mr. Marino was the prosecuting attorney in a robbery case involving John Harrison, who was defended by Mr. Gordon. That trial was reversed, and Mr. Marino was one of the prosecutors in the retrial, in which Mr. Gordon served again as defense counsel. Then, just two months ago, Mr. Marino was the prosecutor in the Harrison murder trial in which, again, Mr. Gordon was the defense counsel. It was at the conclusion of that trial, in the presence of Mr. Marino, that Mr. Gordon was arrested for subornation of perjury, the charge alleged in the indictment for this case. The factual basis for the indictment is based on an allegation that at the robbery retrial of John Harrison, the testimony of two witnesses was perjured testimony resulting from a payoff allegedly by Mr. Gordon. I do not wish to argue how absurd and preposterous that charge is, but—"

Samarkos was quickly interrupted. "Then *don't* argue the absurdity, Mr. Samarkos. Just tell me why I should dismiss Mr. Marino from prosecuting this case."

Samarkos bent his head slightly and smiled. It was a mild rebuke, and he realized it was deserved. "Yes, Your Honor." He then continued. "There are several reasons. First, because Mr. Marino was present when the alleged perjury occurred, he could very well be a witness in this case. That is sufficient in itself. But perhaps a more important reason can be found in the Prosecution Standards of the National District Attorneys Association. Let me quote: 'The prosecutor should excuse himself or herself from any prosecution where personal interests of the prosecutor would cause a fair-minded, objective observer to conclude that the prosecutor's neutrality, judgment, or ability to administer the law in an objective manner may be compromised.'

"Mr. Gordon and Mr. Marino have opposed each other in three recent criminal trials. Of course, this alone, does not support our motion, but these were hotly contested, high-profile, criminal trials. Because of the high stakes, emotions come into play. We believe, as noted in the prosecution standards I just quoted, that a fair-minded, objective observer, could and would conclude that the prosecutor's neutrality, judgment, and ability to administer the law in an objective manner could be compromised. To avoid this, we move that Mr. Marino be removed from prosecuting this case."

Samarkos turned from the lectern and took his seat at the defense table.

Fasi stood at the prosecution table. "Your Honor, we believe our brief conclusively refutes any basis claimed for this motion. There is no legitimacy for a claim that Mr. Marino could or would be a witness in this case, and there is no reasonable argument that his service as prosecutor in this case would breach any standard of the National District Attorneys Association. The defendant is entitled to *counsel* of his choice; he is not entitled to the *prosecutor* of his choice." He then took his seat.

Judge McCabe looked at Samarkos. "Anything else from the defense?"

"No, Your Honor."

Judge McCabe quickly announced his decision. "The motion is denied. Any further motions from either counsel?"

Both counsel replied in the negative, and the judge conferred with the court clerk for a couple of minutes, then announced, "I'm setting the trial for the week of November 17. Is that satisfactory with counsel?"

Scott and Samarkos consulted their calendars and neither found a conflict. Scott thought the five months until trial was a long time to have an indicted lawyer flying around the country appearing as counsel in criminal trials. And he knew there would possibly be delays that would increase that time. But the trial date was set, and he would begin preparations.

Chapter Five

THURSDAY, JUNE 26

Samarkos was in his office a few hours after the motion hearing when he received the phone call. It was expected.

"Hello, Max," he said.

"I've only got a couple minutes," Gordon said. "We're in recess at my trial in Cleveland. Give me an update on the hearing this morning. Did you get that little shithead removed?"

"The motion was denied, as I explained to you that it likely would be," Samarkos replied.

"And I explained to you that you were to get him dismissed. Did you forget?"

"Max, I gave it my best shot. I know you want him off the case, but really, your case is stronger with Marino prosecuting. I know you've had a bad experience opposing him in the Harrison trials, but he's still the least experienced felony prosecutor in the DA's office. Best to have him as lead counsel."

"Let me see if I understand you, Charles. You did not get him removed, and you have no plans to get him removed," Gordon said.

"Unless you know something I don't, we don't have additional grounds for his removal," said Samarkos. "The judge has ruled on it, and further argument will not change the ruling and will only irritate the judge."

"That's it? That's all you've got for me?" Gordon replied in a clearly exasperated tone.

"That's all I have on that issue. But I've received the initial discovery package from the prosecution, and I'm getting to work on that now."

"Don't bother," said Gordon. "If you are the best attorney in Savannah and can't follow simple instructions, apparently there is no one there capable of handling this case. I'll find someone who can. Are you competent enough to submit a motion to withdraw as counsel?"

Samarkos kept his cool. He had dealt with difficult clients many times but few like Max Gordon. Gordon, as the client, had set the fees in this case—a first for Samarkos—and they were quite good. But no fee was sufficient for representing an abusive client the likes of Max Gordon. In fact, rather than being disappointed at losing Max as a client, he felt relieved. He did not lack other well-paying clients.

Samarkos ignored Max's question. "Whoever you hire, Max, should contact me ASAP. The prosecution has provided quite a bit of discovery. They are working on the case as we speak, and your new lawyer needs to get moving. But let me make sure I understand exactly what you want. You want me off the case—and to submit a withdrawal motion, effective immediately."

"Finally, you seem to understand something," Max replied.

"It will be done today, Max," Samarkos said. He hung up the phone and smiled. He would do so with pleasure.

Samarkos prepared the motion, and as it was being typed, he called Scott.

"Thought I would give you a heads-up. I'm submitting a motion to withdraw from the Gordon case—at my client's request."

"Are you at liberty to give me the reason?" asked Scott. "Or did he just dislike you as much as he dislikes me?" Scott said with a chuckle.

"No comment on that, Scott. Let's just say he wasn't happy with the decision on the motion this morning, and we had a mild disagreement on strategy."

"Mild? You got fired over a *mild* disagreement?"

"Maybe we can have a chat about this sometime after this trial is concluded. Right now, I just wanted to let you know I will be off the case as soon as the judge approves my motion to withdraw," Samarkos said.

"Do you know who he's bringing in?" asked Scott.

"No, Gordon didn't tell me who he has in mind," Samarkos replied. "You'll likely find out as soon as I do. Please hold any additional discovery material until we hear. What you've already provided to me, I'll turn over to his new counsel, so you won't have to start over."

"By the way, Charles," Scott said. "The argument you presented about my being disqualified for possibly being a witness concerned me when I first heard it. Initially, I didn't think there were any possible grounds for having me dismissed, but I hadn't thought about the witness argument. I knew he hated my guts for being an arrogant son-of-a-bitch, but that was not going to be enough." Scott chuckled as he spoke.

"So, you heard that. I wasn't sure. You kept walking," Samarkos said.

"I thought it was sort of funny. I'm not exactly in love with Max Gordon either," Scott responded.

"I can understand that," Samarkos said. "And now that we've cleared that up, I'll let you go. I'll send over a copy of my withdrawal motion this afternoon."

"Thanks," Scott said, "for the heads-up."

Chapter Six

Monday, June 30

The following Monday, Scott received a phone call from Fasi. "If you have some time today, stop by my office. I want to discuss the Gordon case."

"I can do it now."

"Good. Come on down."

Scott welcomed the opportunity to visit in Fasi's office. It was a mini-museum of sports memorabilia. The walls were covered with framed and autographed photos of sports legends. Two photos that impressed Scott the most were Braves Hall of Famer Hank Aaron and Braves star pitcher Greg Maddux. Both were pictured in their Braves uniforms, and both photos were signed with bold handwriting in blue ink. Scott was drafted by the Braves in 2001, after his senior year at the University of Alabama, and spent two years on their minor league roster before realizing he wasn't going to make it to the majors. While there, he met Maddux and watched several games in which he pitched. He was sure Maddux would join Aaron in the Hall of Fame someday. The photos brought back some bittersweet memories of his brief stay in the Braves' franchise.

Scott walked down the corridor to Fasi's office, was waved in, and took a seat.

"Anything new on Max Gordon's case since the hearing last week?" Fasi asked.

"Yes, a couple of things. When Samarkos informed Max that he lost the motion to have me dismissed, it upset Max so much he fired Samarkos," Scott said with a grin.

"Fired him? You're kidding!"

"Nope. Samarkos called me that same afternoon, telling me that he and Gordon had a mild disagreement over strategy and at Gordon's demand, Samarkos had just submitted his request to withdraw. I haven't received the judge's action on the request, and no one so far has entered an appearance as substitute counsel. Samarkos told me to hold any further discovery material until the new counsel appears."

"Do you know if he's planning on hiring a local attorney?"

"No, Samarkos said Gordon didn't tell him who he planned to hire."

"I expect he'll bring in someone from out of town. What's going on with your witnesses? They've all been arraigned, haven't they?"

"All except the guy from Colorado, Josh Johnson. He's scheduled for arraignment Wednesday. He's still locked up. Couldn't make bail. Claims he lost all his money in a divorce last year and at a couple of casinos in Black Hawk, Colorado, and he's broke. But I think he's stashed that $250,000 Gordon paid him somewhere, probably down in Mexico or the Caribbean. He just can't get his hands on it now. But that's fine with us. We need to cut a deal for his testimony. A few days in the Chatham County jail should help with that, but we haven't proposed anything yet. He's represented by the public defender."

"What about the other witnesses?"

"The local guy, Patel, was arraigned and is out on bail," Scott replied. "Good that he's out on bail; he's a basket case. Would have to be on suicide watch if in jail, according to his attorney."

"Who's his attorney?"

"Luke Schaub. Luke says Patel's embarrassed, contrite, depressed. Can't believe he could get involved in Gordon's deal. He had a couple of kids to put through college, but he was doing well enough in his business for that. But $250,000—that was just too much and he bit. I want to make a reasonable plea offer. But what's reasonable, Joe? Here's a guy with no record at all. My investigator, Richard Evans, tells me he can't even find a traffic citation. Seemed to be a perfect father and citizen until Max came along."

Fasi folded his arms and then got up from his desk and walked to a window. He had a solemn, pensive expression on his face. He looked out on the street below for a few moments before turning to face Scott.

"Not too unusual, Scott. Money corrupts, especially big money. But let's take a look at all the players in this case. The DA, me, you—we need to all be on the same page. I'm sure you agree that the worst of all defendants in this case is the corruptor-in-chief, Max Gordon. The others must pay for their crimes, but Max should pay the most and feel the full impact of the law. We should make whatever offers are needed to nail him. To convict Max, we need their testimony." Fasi walked back to his desk and sat down.

"Of course," Scott said. "And we'll get it. Max's co-defendant, Wilborn—the delivery guy—has a deal in place in Fulton County for his drug trafficking charges. DeBickero helped him cut a deal on the state charges in exchange for his testimony in our case—a maximum of ten years, and perhaps less, depending on how the judge feels after he gets our report on his cooperation. He's already pleaded guilty but won't be sentenced until after this trial. He's out on bail, with an ankle monitor. We won't have any problem with his testimony. He doesn't have any room to wiggle. The feds could have him locked up for any period of time they wish—ten years to life, and he still faces the charges in this case. And regarding those charges, I want to get a plea out of him soon—lock him in. He's a principal in the perjury subornation charges, same as Max, facing ten years on each. I would like to make an offer now—whatever he gets here to be served concurrently with whatever sentence he gets in Fulton County."

"The defense will have a field day with him on cross, whether or not he testifies with a plea offer in place," Fasi said. "But we can't help that—just something we have to accept. So offer it, if you think that will help your case. And how strong a case do you think you have with those witnesses?"

Scott raised his chin, looking toward the ceiling. After a few moments, he lowered his head and let out a sigh.

"Well let me think about my witnesses," he said with a grimace. "I've got two, who by the time we go to trial, will be admitted perjurers testifying with nice plea deals. And I have one convicted drug dealer, who by the time we go to trial, will also be convicted of two counts of subornation of perjury and two counts of influencing witnesses and also testifying under a plea deal. So it should be a slam dunk." Scott smiled, then laughed at his assessment.

Fasi added his own: "Reminds me of a famous quote by a Marine general during the Korean War—Chesty Puller, I believe it was—'They're on our right, they're on our left, they're in front of us, they're behind us; they can't get away from us this time.'" They both laughed.

"That was my dad's favorite Marine Corps quote, and he had a lot of 'em," said Fasi. "He was in the Marine Corps for two years, got to Vietnam with the First Marine Division just before the division pulled out in 1971. Served the rest of his time at Camp Pendleton, was discharged when his two years were up. And thirty-five years later, he still claims to be a Marine." Fasi smiled as he spoke. Obviously he had fond memories of his dad. He stood up again and went to the window. Without turning to look at Scott, he asked, "Now really, Scott, how do you think the case is shaping up?"

"Seriously, Joe," Scott said, "I think we're in good shape. These witnesses will have a lot of baggage, but I think they'll be believable. We have to take our witnesses as they are. I think I've heard you say that. We'll have to make some deals that I would prefer not to make, but we need to put Max out of action once and for all. We should be able to get ten years for him. He'll lose his license. Wilborn will probably get about six to eight, and he'll also lose his license. All in all, a good result."

Fasi turned once more to Scott. "Then keep on top of it and keep me informed—weekly, if you have anything new. I'll be sitting as second chair, but you'll continue as lead counsel. And let me know if you need any additional help."

The meeting was over. As far as Scott was concerned it was a very satisfactory meeting. It confirmed that he would remain as lead counsel. He was also happy that Fasi would be sitting with him. He hoped Fasi would take charge of jury selection, the part of a criminal trial where Scott felt he was weakest and in which he knew Fasi excelled. But the trial itself would be his.

Chapter Seven

Thursday, July 3

Scott was in his office early Thursday morning, taking care of some pressing last-minute matters. He would be leaving later that afternoon with Jennifer for Hilton Head to begin a long weekend. Scott had been looking forward to this Fourth-of-July weekend for quite some time. His schedule had him working at least one full day on most weekends since the middle of May. His visits with Jennifer to her parents' home were always special. Her parents were gracious hosts during the day and left them to be alone for the evenings. Sometimes it was for a concert at Sea Pines Resort, other times just a stroll along the beach with a blanket, looking for a quiet place in the dunes to lie down together and listen to the churning of the waves.

Scott had a light work schedule the following week, but there was an important motion hearing midweek. He hoped nothing new would come up in the next few hours that could not be put off until at least Monday. It had happened before when he and Jennifer were planning a weekend at Hilton Head. When the phone rang, and he heard Charles Samarkos on the other end, he was sure it was about to happen again.

"Scott, Charles here. Hope your morning is going well. Ready for a nice Fourth?"

"Good morning, Charles. My morning is going fine; I hope you aren't calling with something to spoil it."

"No, just wanted to tell you I received a call from James Colosimo. He reports that he's been hired as defense counsel by Max Gordon. He's arriving from Atlanta on Monday to discuss the case with me and pick up the discovery material. He mentioned that he'd like to meet with you before he returned. Asked that I give you a call to see if you had some time Monday afternoon. I told him I would check and call him back."

"I'll make time." Scott looked at his calendar. Monday afternoon was clear. "Tell him two o'clock works for me. Is he an Atlanta lawyer?"

"Yes, criminal defense. Lots of white collar crime, major drug cases."

"Do you know him?" asked Scott.

"Met him several years ago at a Georgia Criminal Defense Lawyers conference in Atlanta. He was on a panel discussion about some topic I can't remember. But I remember Colosimo—he took command of the panel and spoke a lot about himself and his background. Very colorful guy. Originally from Chicago. Proudly claims 'Diamond Jim' Colosimo was his great-grandfather."

"'Diamond Jim' Colosimo? Who was that?"

"He was an Al Capone-era Mafioso. In the twenties—early prohibition time."

"That's someone he's proud to claim as a relative?"

"Oh, yes, very much so," said Samarkos. "He even dresses the part. Diamonds on the fingers of both hands. Passes out business cards with his photo, and a diamond in each corner. He's an interesting guy. Got me curious about the great-grandfather claim, so after I got back from Atlanta, I checked out 'Diamond Jim' Colosimo on the Internet. I had heard of 'Diamond Jim' *Brady* but not 'Diamond

Jim' *Colosimo*. But there it was, along with a photo, and he had a big—I mean *really* big and wide—black moustache, just like our panel guy. The website reported that 'Diamond Jim' wore white linen suits, and I recalled our speaker was also dressed in a white linen suit. But I had no way of checking his claim that it was his great-grandfather."

"I wonder how such a guy from Chicago found his way to Atlanta," said Scott.

"Oh, he explained that. As I said, he took over the panel, spent half the time talking about himself and how he became a lawyer. He said proudly that he attended Atlanta Law School. It's out of business now, but it was a long-standing law school until sometime in the 1990s. It was accredited by the Georgia Board of Bar Examiners, and graduates didn't have to take the bar exam—get your diploma and you were admitted to the bar. James didn't say that's why he attended, but it's my guess for a good reason for a guy from Chicago—or anywhere else—to attend. And once he was a member of the Georgia Bar, it was easy to make a decision to stay. In any case, he was pretty proud of his law school. Mentioned that several members of Congress, six governors and two chief justices of the Georgia Supreme Court had degrees from there."

"Well, that shows how little I know," Scott said. "Never even heard of it."

"You may hear more. He's not only proud but loud. You are going to enjoy the trial, Scott," Samarkos said, with a laugh.

"Well, the trial's not about Atlanta Law School and 'Diamond Jim.' It's about a low-life named Max Gordon, and yes, I'm going to enjoy it. Are you glad you're out of it?" Scott asked.

"You betcha! Nice talking, Scott," Samarkos said as they hung up.

Scott was curious. *Who was this guy from Atlanta, and what were his qualifications that made him attractive to Max Gordon?* Both had a Chicago connection, but other than that, Scott could only guess.

He pulled up the lawyer listings on the Georgia Bar website. Yes, it showed James A. Colosimo, graduate of Atlanta Law School—in good standing, no disciplinary action on his record. Business address on West Peachtree Street; email address, Jim@diamondjimlaw.com. *He really does like that name*, Scott mused.

Scott wanted more information on this new attorney who had taken on the defense of Max Gordon. He decided to call his former mentor, Grady Wilder, in Atlanta. Grady was an experienced assistant DA and Scott's supervising attorney when Scott was a senior clinic student at Savannah Law, interning at the Chatham County DA's office. Scott was assisting Grady on the initial John Harrison robbery case, which was to be prosecuted by Grady and defended by Max Gordon. Grady had accepted a position with the U.S. Attorney in Atlanta, but his departure coincided with the start of the robbery trial. When the judge denied a motion for a continuance, and no assistant DA was available who was familiar with the case, the DA decided to let Scott prosecute the case. It was very unexpected, even a bit freakish the way it happened, but Grady had trained him well and the prosecution was successful. Scott felt very indebted to Grady, and they had maintained close contact since Grady left for Atlanta.

Scott placed the call and Grady answered. After the usual pleasantries, Scott made his inquiry. "Do you know an Atlanta attorney by the name of James Colosimo?"

"Diamond Jim!" Grady exclaimed.

"So you know him," Scott laughed.

"Oh yes, all of us here in the criminal side of the office know 'Diamond Jim.' Why do you ask?"

"He's now the defense counsel for Max Gordon," Scott replied. Grady was familiar with the Gordon case. He and Scott had discussed it several times since Gordon was arrested in early May.

"Oh, man, you are in for a trip. When did this happen?" Grady asked.

"Today's the first I heard of it," replied Scott. "Got a call from Gordon's old counsel, Charles Samarkos. What do you know about this guy?"

"I've never had a case against him, but several of the others in the office have. They say he's a fairly good attorney in the courtroom. Knows his evidence, knows the law, very good cross-examiner. But man, is he weird. Let me correct that. I don't know if he's weird or just prefers to give that impression. He practices law Chicago-style, if you know what I mean. Did you pull up his website?"

"No, not yet."

"It's interesting," Grady said. "He's the only licensed attorney for his firm, but he lists two from his office as 'law school graduates.' They aren't listed as paralegals, just 'staff members.' The truth is, they're both disbarred attorneys. One had a criminal law practice here in Atlanta before he was disbarred. I don't know where the other one came from. I guess they do his investigations or whatever mischief that needs to be done. I've only run into him a couple of times, so I can't say I really know him, but those who do claim he's a classic bullshit artist. He likes to talk about his outlaw relatives, going back to Al Capone time. Apparently there was a 'Diamond Jim' relative connected to the Chicago underworld some years ago."

"Yes, I heard that from Samarkos," Scott said. "Samarkos said he met Colosimo several years ago at a conference where he appeared on a panel. Spent most of his panel time talking about himself and his family history. Claimed that the original 'Diamond Jim' Colosimo was his great-grandfather. I've been wondering what psychological problem would make a person, especially an attorney, claim to the world that he comes from a long line of crooks and bootleggers."

"Might not be a psychological problem at all, Scott," Grady responded. "May be a clever promotion. Think about it. A crook is seeking a lawyer. Here's one he can identify with—comes from a family of crooks. Another thing in his promotional arsenal is a nightclub restaurant he owns out at Buckhead. He named it 'Colosimo's.' It's famous for its 1920s decor. It has a photo on its menu of a restaurant in Chicago by the same name, which according to the text under the photo, was owned in the 1920s by 'Diamond Jim Colosimo.' Nice steakhouse. I've been there a couple of times. The entryway has a photo of the original 'Diamond Jim' with his biography underneath. The bio claims he died in a hail of gunfire as he was leaving his restaurant, by someone tied to the mob. It's a very large photo, maybe three feet by five, in a fancy wooden frame. Atlanta's 'Diamond Jim' tries to look the same—slicked-back hair style, big black moustache, diamonds on the fingers. So he's pretty well known in Atlanta as one of the go-to guys for people in trouble who have money. He gets the big-stake cases. Doesn't surprise me that Max Gordon hired him. He's a clever shyster—as shady a character as Max Gordon and just as dangerous."

"Thanks for the warning," Scott said. "I'll watch my back."

"Watch your front, too," Grady said. "He's not only weird, but he's a genuine asshole—the real McCoy. He will likely insult you early on. Every prosecutor here who's had a case against him says he did, usually at the first meeting. Apparently he wants the prosecutor to get angry at him—anger that can lead to dumb mistakes. Insulting the prosecutor seems to be part of his professional MO."

"So, a weird, genuine asshole. Look's like I'm in for a fun afternoon next Monday. When are you getting back to Savannah for a weekend? There're some new Moon River brews we need to check out."

"Saint Patrick's Day for sure, but that's a long way off. Maybe I can get down there on a long weekend this fall. I love the town—really miss it."

As soon as they hung up, Scott pulled up Colosimo's law firm website. The website opened with a flash of falling diamonds followed by a large photo of Colosimo, in a diamond-shaped frame. And just below the photo in bold print:

> **I'm "Diamond Jim" Colosimo, and I'm pleased and proud to have one of the most successful criminal defense firms in the nation. With our highly experienced staff, we use a teamwork approach that is an integral feature of our office culture and the cornerstone of our success. We attack your problem aggressively 24/7. We have an expansive office, situated high in the Atlanta skyline. Call the Colosimo Law Firm—Atlanta's big-winner team—for an appointment.**

The "highly experienced staff" seemed to consist of the two men and two female secretaries. There were small snapshot photos of the secretaries, with their names below. The men appeared in larger photos, but still smaller than Colosimo's. Beneath each was his name, followed by "Staff Assistant" with a notation "Law School Graduate." There was no claim that either was a member of any bar.

The younger man, "Anderson McDowell," appeared to be in his mid-30s. The other, "Thomas J. Reid," appeared to be a few years older. Neither was smiling. Scott closed the website. The meeting Monday would be interesting.

Chapter Eight

Monday, July 7

Scott was up early as usual, sitting at his kitchen table with a steaming cup of coffee and the morning newspaper in front of him—his morning ritual. He had enjoyed another great weekend with Jennifer at Hilton Head, returning after a late Sunday afternoon cookout in the family backyard, where Jennifer's father took charge of the grill. This time it was red snapper, marinated and grilled whole, one of her father's specialties—and Scott's favorite.

Scott arrived back at his apartment about 9:00 p.m. Sunday night and turned on his TV. He was hoping to catch the last few minutes of the Braves-Astros game, which started at 5:35 p.m. To his delight, the game was still on, with the score tied 6-6. Then it went into extra innings—the tenth, eleventh . . . and on until the *seventeenth*, with Scott enjoying every minute of the great defensive struggle. Then, in the bottom of the seventeenth, Braves first baseman Mark Teixeira drilled a single, deep to left field, scoring Gregor Blanco and winning the game for the Braves. For Scott, a perfect ending to a perfect weekend.

Though Scott already knew the outcome, it was still a pleasure to read the sports commentary in the morning, so he lingered a bit longer than usual with his paper and coffee. He would be in the office soon enough, back in the grind, making phone calls, reading police reports, and preparing responses to motions. When he had finished the sports section, he turned to other news and didn't find much of interest—two retired Turkish generals failed in a coup attempt and another story of a possible federal bailout for Fannie Mae and Freddie Mac as their share prices continued to plummet. He turned to the automobile classified section even though he was not in the market to buy or sell. He was the proud owner of a black 1984 Z28 Camaro—his pride and joy and the only thing of significant value that he owned. It was equipped with a 305-cubic-inch V-8 engine that produced 150 horsepower, a three-piece spoiler, and aluminum five-spoke wheels. He maintained it in showroom condition—and when not in use, always kept it secure with a steering wheel lock. He had no plans to sell, but he remained curious of its value and what other Camaros were selling for.

There were no new Camaro listings that day. Scott folded the paper, picked up his briefcase, and drove to his office.

A few minutes after 2:00 p.m., Scott received a call that he was expecting.

"There is a Mr. Colosimo to see you," Mary Greenfield, the receptionist, said when Scott answered.

"Tell him to slip you a diamond and send him down," said Scott.

"I'm sorry, could you repeat that?"

"Did he give you a business card?"

"Yes."

"Look at it. What do you see?" asked Scott.

There was a pause. Then a laugh from Mary. "OK, I get it. I'll see if he has one for me. Two carats or more. But in any case, I'm sending him down now," she said.

Scott stood beside his office door to welcome his guest. Colosimo was dressed in a white linen suit and a bolo tie. The tie had a silver adjusting clip decorated with small diamonds, and a braided black leather string with silver aiguillettes also encrusted with small diamonds. He was not tall, perhaps an inch or so less than six feet, but he had a girth that made up for it. He had a full head of black hair, dropping down to his collar in the back and almost to his ear lobes on the side. A thick, broad, rectangular moustache covered a substantial portion of his face. Except that it was black, it had the appearance of a badly adjusted surgical mask. Hard-soled shoes, or more likely boots, made a loud clomping noise as he approached.

Scott extended his hand. "Scott Marino."

"James Colosimo. My friends call me 'Jim—Diamond Jim,'" Colosimo replied. As he extended his arm to shake Scott's hand, his French cuffs with diamond and gold cufflinks, jumped out from his coat sleeve, as if it were a practiced motion.

Scott considered the response but doubted he would ever call this visitor "Diamond Jim." He closed the door and motioned with his hand, inviting Colosimo to a chair just across from his desk.

"I understand you have taken over the Gordon case from Charles Samarkos," Scott said.

"Yes. Charles has been helpful. Gave me a quick briefing on the case. I had a chance to read his motion to have you dismissed from the case. And I'm curious: Why are you fighting that so hard?" Colosimo asked.

"Fighting it? There's nothing to fight. It's already been decided by the judge."

"I think you know what I mean—it's not too difficult to understand, is it?" Colosimo said slowly, emphasizing each word.

Scott ignored the snide remark, but he had no intention of being quizzed by this visitor. He had extended the invitation to visit as a professional courtesy, not as an opportunity to be insulted. *So, insults really are part of his MO*, Scott thought. He would cut this short. He stood up and faced Colosimo.

"I assume you have filed a notice of your appearance with the court. Do you have any questions related to the administration of the case? I'm sure Charles informed you that the trial is scheduled for the week of November 17. Judge McCabe's courtroom is Courtroom K. He usually begins promptly at nine."

"No, I have no administrative questions. I assume that even down here in Chatham County you follow the Georgia Superior Court Rules. And the Georgia Evidence Code. I've been trying criminal cases in Georgia for twenty years. I'm sure by the time the trial concludes, you will see that I'm quite familiar with them. I know you're young and inexperienced. Charles tells me you've been prosecuting less than two years. I recall when I was a young defense counsel just starting out. Like you, I didn't understand some of the law I was dealing with. But the problem was, I also didn't understand that I didn't understand. So I made some mistakes."

Scott was standing and looking at the narrowed eyes of his visitor, still seated. Scott realized Colosimo was in some sort of a lecture mood, mixed with what would likely include a few insults, as Grady had warned. He could just order him out—which was tempting—but he decided to listen. But damned if he would do so standing. He sat back down, and Colosimo continued.

"We've all made mistakes. Your mistakes in this case are multiple, beginning with your failure to accept the fact that you should be disqualified from this case. And that's only the beginning. The bigger error is charging Max Gordon with a crime committed only by that drug pusher and money launderer from Macon. Clarence Wilborn and Clarence Wilborn alone should be charged with this crime. It's prosecutorial misconduct that you are charging Mr. Gordon. We consider it a personal vendetta. But there is another big mistake, a mistake that even someone with your limited knowledge of the law should recognize. You can't prove that *anyone* actually committed perjury. Surely you are aware of the two-witness rule. You may have two witnesses, but you don't have two witnesses to perjury. Just how do you expect to prove your case, Mr. Marino?"

Scott recalled the warning that Colosimo would likely aim an insult or two his way, but he was really surprised at his blatant nastiness. "A few minutes ago," Scott replied, "you claimed to be familiar with the court rules. Apparently you have forgotten. It's called a trial, Mr. Colosimo. A jury trial, and you'll have to attend to find out."

"And you would be wise to take my advice and cut your losses. Wilborn should be your target. Carefully consider it, Mr. Marino. My roots go back to Chicago. My great grandfather was the original 'Diamond Jim' Colosimo. He got rich running brothels—two hundred of them. Also ran one of the most famous and profitable restaurants in Chicago—Colosimo's."

Scott was tempted once more to interrupt Colosimo and direct him to leave his office. But he was curious as to where this legal dolt was heading with this tale. He decided to let him run on. Perhaps he would learn something of the defense strategy. Scott sat back in his chair and focused his eyes on the character sitting across from him.

Colosimo continued. "That was the Al Capone era. I'm a student of the history of that time period. I've read everything that's ever been published and much that hasn't been—accounts handed down in the family. There's one particular story that you would be well-advised to research. There may be a lesson in it for you. It involved a young, hard-charging prosecutor—an assistant state attorney in Chicago by the name of William McSwiggin. He was about your age and assigned to pursue an indictment against Al Capone for killing a guy in a South Side bar. And he did so with vigor. You may want to take a look and see how that helped his career. Well, enough advice for now." Colosimo paused for a moment, then began again. "Now one last thing—"

Scott cut him off. "I agree, Mr. Colosimo. That's enough for now." Scott stood, walked quickly to the door and opened it. "I'll see you in court, sir, November 17, nine sharp."

Chapter Nine

Tuesday, July 8

Scott was to meet Jennifer at the Library Bar and Grill at 6:00 p.m. They had plans for dinner and a movie. They had discussed two movies, both just released the previous week: *Wanted*, an R-rated, violent-action movie, and *WALL·E*, a G-rated Disney Pixar adventure film. Neither was in the mood for a movie of bloody violence that *Wanted* promised, but a G-rated Disney movie did not seem all that appealing either. They would discuss it at dinner.

Scott arrived first and walked to the bar. He did not see anyone tending the bar as he took his seat, but he knew Juri was not far off. He knocked the bar top with his knuckles a couple of times, and playfully yelled, "Service, service!" Then he turned to face the doorway and watch for Jennifer. Soon a cold mug of beer was sliding gracefully down the bar from about twelve feet away. It stopped right in front of Scott.

"Perfect, perfect!" Juri said, standing at the end of the bar. Scott turned just in time to see Juri kiss his forearm twice and say, "I'm sooo good!"

"Glad to see you in a good mood, after that disaster of a ball game by the Braves last night," Scott said.

"Ah, don't bring that up—one hit—one lousy hit from the whole team. With Chipper Jones being the only guy hitting over three hundred, what do you expect? What's wrong, Scott?"

"Like I said last time you asked, nothing's wrong except hitting, pitching, and fielding. Maybe they excel at base running," Scott said with a grin.

"Base running! How would we know? They have to get on base first! No, Scott, I gave up on this gang a couple weeks ago," Juri said.

"Did you see the night game on Sunday?" Scott asked.

"Yeah, seventeen innings. Almost midnight before Teixeira singles to bring in Blanco. Took 'em seventeen innings!"

"So, you watched 'til almost midnight. Admit it, Juri, you really haven't given up on 'em," Scott said.

"No, you got me, Scott. I guess the Braves are in my soul. Division championships fifteen years straight. No one will ever top that. I can't give up on 'em, but they are making me hurt right now."

"Me too," Scott said. "But they'll come back. Maybe not in time for this season, but they'll come back. Winners always do." Scott glanced at the entryway and saw Jennifer. "Speaking of winners, I see one heading our way."

Scott stood, gave Jennifer a quick kiss, and they both took a seat at the bar.

"Well hello, Jennifer. I've got a good one for you," Juri said, with a grin. He was immediately interrupted by Scott.

"Your manners, Juri, your manners. Get Jennifer something—her favorite, if you recall."

"Sure, sure, sorry," Juri said, turning and walking over to some bar supplies a few feet away. In just a few moments he was back with Jennifer's drink. The grin returned, along with a twinkle in his eye. He turned his head side to side, looking to make sure he had both Scott's and Jennifer's attention before beginning once again.

"This blonde was trying to sell her old car. Problem was it had 250,000 miles on it. She told her friend about her problem. 'Oh, I know a mechanic who can fix that,' her friend said. 'He can turn that odometer back. That'll help you sell it.' He wrote the mechanic's address on a card. 'Thanks, I'll do it,' the blonde said. A couple weeks later, friend sees her, and she's driving the same old car. 'Still trying to sell the old car?' the friend asked."

Juri took a step back, carefully surveying his listeners before continuing.

"'No,' the blonde says. 'Why should I? It only has 10,000 miles on it!'"

Juri's enthusiastic laughter after his own jokes was always contagious. Scott and Jennifer joined in, but at the same time Scott gave him a thumbs down with both hands. It did not deter Juri. "What's the difference between a lawyer and a catfish?" he asked, but before anyone could answer, he said, "One's a slimy, bottom-dwelling, scum sucker. The other's a fish." Juri continued laughing—he had not stopped laughing from his first joke.

"That's awful, Juri—also, old and worn," Scott said. "But why do you make fun of us? We're just trying to make an honest living. And here's something to consider—saw it on a bumper sticker this morning. 'If you think lawyer jokes are funny, next time you're in a jam call a comedian.' What do you think of that?"

"Think of that? Well, it reminds me of another story. Woman lawyer walks into a bar holding a duck—"

"No! Enough! A curse on the Braves tonight if you continue. Jennifer and I are having dinner here, and any more we'll both lose our appetites. Bring me the tab when you figure it up."

"Tab's on me if the Braves beat the Dodgers tonight and double on you if they lose," Juri replied.

"You're on," Scott said. He reached for Jennifer's hand and they left the bar for the Library dining room, just around the corner from the bar. The restaurant was not crowded, and they found their favorite table, a corner booth.

Once they were seated, Jennifer said, "Didn't you want to hear about the woman lawyer and the duck?" She had a playful smile on her face.

"Not tonight. He'll tell it the next time we're here, and I wanted to tell you about a visit I had with the new attorney for Max Gordon."

"Diamond Jim? You told me that Charles Samarkos had briefed you about him and his colorful lifestyle. Did he live up to it?"

"Sure did," said Scott. "He's even weirder than Samarkos led me to believe. And he plays the part, down to his attire. He was wearing a white linen suit and a black bolo tie. Black hair and moustache—moustache covered half his face, wide and rectangular. And diamonds. Diamonds on his tie, diamond cuff links, diamonds on his fingers. I'm not sure, but I think he had diamonds on every finger, both hands. You remember my friend, Grady Wilder, don't you? My supervisor when I was interning at the DA's office?"

"I never met him, but you spoke of him often," Jennifer said.

"He's a federal prosecutor in Atlanta now. I called him to see what he knew of Colosimo. Grady said his weirdness is part of his PR. He may in fact be weird, but it gets him a lot of publicity—and is attractive to the criminal element. Meet him, or see him or just hear of him, and you remember. Psychologically, I guess, diamonds mean success, and success means he's a winner. Seems to work for him. Grady says he's one of the go-to criminal defense lawyers in Atlanta and pretty good in the courtroom. But weirdness is not the only trait that sets him apart. He's got the personality of a snake."

"You found that out in the first visit?"

"Yes. He goes out of his way to insult. Grady warned me about it, so I was on guard not to lose my cool."

A waitress came for their order, and they realized that while they had been talking neither had even picked up the menu. They took a brief glance at it, and both quickly ordered; they were eager to return to their conversation.

Scott continued. "As I was saying, he has the personality of a snake and a tongue just as venomous. He said I was young and inexperienced and had already made multiple mistakes. He may be correct on all points, but it was also an obvious attempt to insult. He listed three mistakes I had already made, the first, not accepting that I should be disqualified from prosecuting the case. That's the motion Samarkos made and Judge McCabe denied. Then he said that I should realize that Max Gordon did not commit any crime and that it was 'prosecutorial misconduct' to charge him. Finally, he added that even with my 'limited knowledge of the law'—mentioned that a couple of times—I should understand that I couldn't prove perjury because of the two-witness rule. I suppose if Grady hadn't told me that insulting the prosecutor was part of his MO, I may have gotten angry. Obviously that's what he was hoping for. Fact is, I thought he was funny, in a pathetic sort of way."

"I see what you mean by 'personality of a snake'," Jennifer said. "But snakes can be dangerous. Teamed up with his client Max Gordon, he could be *really* dangerous. I don't see it as 'funny' at all. You better watch your back."

"Same advice I got from Grady," Scott said. "But let me tell you about the end of the conversation with this guy. He said he was a student of history of the Al Capone era, and there was a story I should check out. Seems there was a young, hard-charging Chicago prosecutor by the name of William McSwiggin, about my age. He was assigned to prosecute an indictment against Al Capone for a murder in a Chicago bar. Said I should look it up to see how that had helped his career. That's all he said about it. I haven't had a chance to check it out, but I am curious. I've read a few stories about Al Capone and his gang, but don't recall anything about a McSwiggin."

"Let me check it out. I'll be over at the law library all day tomorrow, working on my ARP. I'll see what I can find about the career of McSwiggin. Sally Waters, one of the research librarians, has been helping me. She's good. If I can't find anything, I'm sure she can."

"Thanks. And enough about Gordon's weird attorney. How is the trip planning coming?" Scott asked.

Jennifer and her family were going to Europe in a few weeks. It was the main topic of discussion during the visit to Hilton Head the past weekend. Jennifer gave him an update on their plans. Their meal was served, and they continued the conversation without mentioning again the Gordon case or "Diamond Jim." Afterwards, neither *Wanted* nor *WALL·E* seemed appealing.

"I have a better idea," Jennifer said. "Let's just go to my place. I'm sure we can find something to do more interesting than either movie."

Chapter Ten

Wednesday, July 9

Scott arrived for work early the next morning. He had a busy schedule for the day, which included a briefing for Joe Fasi on his meeting with Colosimo Monday afternoon. Scott was still digesting the contents of the investigative file that had been prepared by GBI agent Carl DeBickero. It was several inches thick and contained quite a bit of criminal investigation jargon that was not familiar to Scott. Much of that concerned the transfer of payoff money. The delivery of the cash from Wilborn to Patel and Johnson was easy to follow, though Scott still wondered why Wilborn, with a half million in cash and driving alone across the country in his SUV, didn't just skip the country. That could be expected from such a lowlife crook. After all, before hooking up with Max Gordon for the Harrison trial, Wilborn was just skirting by with a failing law practice conducted from a small office located between a tattoo parlor and pawn shop in a dingy strip mall on the south side of Macon.

The money transfer between Senator Harrison, Gordon, the drug cartel, and the eventual cash transfer to Wilborn, was complicated. He had discussed that with Carl, but even Carl had questions still to be answered. Carl had been unable to interview Senator

Harrison, who was now hospitalized from another stroke from which he was unlikely to recover. Carl had obtained court orders for a massive amount of phone records, but there were no text messages in the records. These players had been too smart for that. And the phone records contained little more than originating and answering phone numbers, dates, and length of calls. That could be valuable in some criminal investigations, but not here, as Scott already had three of the four indicted defendants ready to testify—or they soon would be. Hopefully he would not need this extensive—and rather elusive—evidence from the investigative report. But he was still working hard to make sure he understood as much as possible and wasn't missing something.

Midmorning, Scott received a phone call from Jennifer. "I was able to track William McSwiggin," she said. "He wasn't such an obscure person after all. I admit I'd never heard of him, but there's quite a bit about him on the Internet."

"Tell me about him," Scott said.

"The research your new friend, Diamond Jim, recommended was about McSwiggin's career, right?"

"Right—said I could learn something from researching his career," Scott replied.

"Didn't take long. His career was cut short," Jennifer said.

"Meaning what?"

"Meaning that for a young prosecutor, he should not have been saddled with prosecuting Al Capone for murder."

"You're not making sense," Scott said. "Tell me about his *career*. That was the thing 'my new friend,' as you call him, said I could learn a lot from."

"And that's what I'm trying to tell you. Prosecuting Al Capone was not a good career start for William McSwiggin—he was murdered. And they never discovered who murdered him. Of course, Capone was one of the suspects, because McSwiggin was actively pursuing him. But Capone was never charged—no one was. Scott, I'm not joking; I think this is serious. That guy was trying to send you a message—you pursue Gordon and you'll end up like McSwiggin—dead!"

Scott listened carefully to Jennifer. If her research was correct—and he was sure it was— Colosimo was indeed trying to send a message. During their brief meeting on Monday afternoon, Colosimo named three major mistakes Scott had made, and the first mistake he mentioned was not disqualifying himself from prosecuting Gordon. At the time, Scott thought he was merely trying to anger him by insulting him. But now, considering the McSwiggin tale and his insistence that Scott research McSwiggin's 'career,' perhaps it was much more than an insult—a warning for Scott to step aside. He certainly could not discount that possibility. After all, he was dealing with a genuine weirdo obsessed with Chicago's gangland history of the 1920s.

Scott noted the concern in Jennifer's voice, and he did not want to further alarm her. "Oh, it was just part of his shtick," Scott said. "Wanted to send me on a wild goose chase. And even if he was trying to send a message, it's merely a lame attempt to frighten me. It failed. End of story."

"Scott, that may not be the end of the story. He really may have something evil in mind. I'm concerned."

"I wish you weren't; it really should be of no concern. The guy is just weird. But if it will ease your concern, I'll check him out—see if there is any violence in his past." Scott had heard nothing from Grady to indicate Colosimo may be prone to violence. His weirdness was a PR ploy. He hoped this promise to check on him would satisfy Jennifer. It didn't.

"Scott, I'm really concerned. I want you to tell your supervisor about it. Promise me."

"I will, Jennifer. In fact, I have a meeting with him this afternoon."

After the call, Scott sat at his desk for several minutes, just staring across the room at a bare wall. He wished that he had never mentioned the McSwiggin story to her. He could see that she was upset. But it was absurd to think this was an actual threat on his life. Yes, Colosimo may have been trying to anger and frighten him, but surely he did not expect Scott to drop out of the case. And *murder*? Ridiculous. However, he had promised Jennifer he would check him out. He placed a call to Atlanta.

"Grady, when you briefed me on 'Diamond Jim' Colosimo, you made it clear that he was one weird dude, but you never indicated any violence in his background. May I assume that there is none?"

"No, of course you can't make such an assumption. Didn't you listen to my lecture on assumptions?" Grady replied, with a laugh. "But I haven't heard of any. Of course, I've been here less than two years. Can't say I know a lot about his past. But violence? I think I would have heard if there was any. He's a pretty talked-about guy. As I said, he's weird, but his weirdness is deliberate. Why do you ask?"

"I met with him briefly in my office Monday afternoon. He was everything you said, and he did his best to insult me. But he went further. Ever heard of an Al Capone-era prosecutor by the name of William McSwiggin?"

"Can't say that I have," replied Grady.

"Well, Colosimo told me I could learn a lot by checking out a young prosecutor who was assigned to prosecute an indictment against Al Capone for murder. His name was William McSwiggin. Colosimo said I should check out how this helped his career. I mentioned it to Jennifer and she checked it out. Seems McSwiggin didn't have a career after the Capone assignment. He was murdered. Capone was a suspect, but it was never proved. No one was ever charged. I think Colosimo was attempting two things: get me angry, as you said he would try, and to frighten me. He did neither. I think he's a clown. But Jennifer's concerned—made me promise I would check out the guy for violence. So, as I promised, I'm checking it out."

"Well, I don't have any knowledge of any violence, but this guy's not a *clown*, Scott, if you are using that in the sense of his being stupid. In fact, he's a shrewd Chicago-style lawyer. I think he's capable of almost any shenanigan—inside and outside the courtroom, but I doubt that violence is part of his practice. Tell Jennifer that Grady said not to worry."

"Will do. Thanks, Grady."

Scott was in Fasi's office at 3:00 p.m. for the scheduled briefing on the Gordon case. There were some preliminary questions about Scott's case load, which now was one of the heaviest in the entire felony division. Fasi suggested that Scott try to unload more cases via pretrial agreements. He was aware that Scott preferred to take his cases to trial, and Fasi was insisting that he make better use of plea agreements.

"It's a matter of good case management, Scott. We aren't getting any more prosecutors in the felony division any time soon, but the number of new cases is increasing each month. We need to move them. I want you to bring me a list of the cases you have scheduled for trial for August and September. We'll discuss them and together come up with a satisfactory plea agreement for each. How about Friday morning? Do you have an hour or so?"

"Sure. I have a hearing in a drug case at nine, but I should be out by ten or ten-thirty. How about eleven?" Scott said.

"Eleven is good," said Fasi. "I want you to have a proposed pretrial for each case. We'll discuss and together finalize it. Bring your October docket also. And if we need more time, we can finish early next week. Now, what's the latest with the Gordon case?"

"Couple of things. Johnson—the guy from Colorado—was arraigned last week on both perjury and conspiracy to commit perjury. He's represented by the PD and still hasn't made bail. He's got that $250,000 stashed somewhere, so he'll eventually make bail—or maybe he won't. If it's not in a bank and he has it stashed somewhere, he'll have to get help to get it. Who's he gonna trust with that sum of money? I think he'll remain in jail a while. Bail's set at $25,000."

"I take it he entered a 'not guilty' plea to both?" Fasi asked.

"Yes," Scott said. "I contacted his attorney about a deal for a guilty plea to the conspiracy charge and dismissing the perjury charge. I explained he could get ten years for perjury but only five for the conspiracy. I offered him three years. His attorney is new to the PD office and wants some time to consider the plea before making a recommendation to his client. I think the offer is more than fair, considering the gravity of the crimes that were committed. But I need his testimony, so I may have to give a bit—perhaps suspend a portion. We'll see."

"What about the other perjurer—the local guy?" asked Fasi.

"I offered him the same deal. He hasn't gotten back with me," Scott said. "And that's about all that's new with the witnesses, but there's something new with the defendant—Gordon has a new defense counsel."

"Local attorney?" asked Fasi.

"No, from Atlanta—James Colosimo, but he prefers to go by the name of 'Diamond Jim' Colosimo—and he's just the sort of guy you would expect to team up with Max Gordon."

Scott related to Fasi all he had learned about "Diamond Jim" from Samarkos and Grady—all the weirdness, as well as Grady's assessment that despite his weirdness, he's a fairly savvy trial attorney. He described Colosimo's law firm's website with the two "law school graduates," his garish personal appearance, and his snarky conversation at the meeting Monday afternoon. He also told of his comment that the two-witness rule would prevent proof of perjury. Finally, Scott recounted Colosimo's suggestion that he research what had happened to William McSwiggin's career after his attempt to prosecute Capone.

Fasi was seated comfortably in his chair and listened silently until Scott told of Jennifer's research, which revealed that McSwiggin was murdered. Then, he quickly sat upright, bristling with anger.

"Give me Colosimo's phone number!" Fasi said. "I'm going to call that schmuck right now. He needs to be put on notice that he better keep his Chicago-style lawyering in Atlanta because we're not going to have it in Chatham County. He won't be playing that game here."

"Joe, I don't think that's the best way to handle this guy," Scott said. "In fact, that's probably what he's hoping for—get us pissed off, angry, concentrating on things that are not related to the case. It's part of his MO, according to Grady. I think it best to ignore him. Grady says there is no sign of violence in the guy. I don't know anything about the background of his two disbarred staff associates, but we can have Carl check them out. He doesn't scare me, and I don't want him thinking he does. Let's just ignore it for now."

Fasi stood up from his desk, walked to a window and looked out without speaking. Several moments later he turned and faced Scott.

"You are probably right, Scott. As you saw, it worked!" Fasi began to laugh. "The son-of-a-bitch got me steamed up, and I haven't even met him! Played us—well, played me—like a violin. He may be weird, but as Grady warned us, a savvy guy. We not only have to watch him, but we have to watch ourselves."

Fasi looked over at Scott and said, "About his question of how you'll prove the perjury, Scott. It does present a problem with the two-witness rule. I tried a case a few years ago, an armed robbery down on River Street. The witness testified he was at a restaurant in Macon with the defendant when the armed robbery occurred. We charged him with perjury. We produced two witnesses who testified that he was actually in Savannah—and we got a conviction. Classic example of the two-witness rule. But the facts of this case are so different in applying the two-witness rule. Patel and Johnson testified that the defendant they were viewing in the courtroom was not the guy they had seen with the gun. What's your proof they were lying?"

"True, there is a problem," Scott said, "but if they accept our plea offer—and I think they will—we'll have their confession from the witness stand that they lied—that's one witness. The statute also provides that perjury can be proved with one witness, corroborated by circumstances. That's our case—we have the corroborating circumstances. We have Patel's testimony at the first trial that John Harrison was the man with the gun—we'll introduce the transcript. Josh Johnson arrived at the trial too late to testify—the jury was already in deliberations when he got to the courthouse. But he saw Harrison in the courtroom, seated at the defense table, and both Daniel Mackay and Richard Evans heard Johnson say, 'That's the man.' I'll have both testify. And we have the *promise* to lie for $250,000. That should count for something. It will be up to the jury to determine if this is sufficient corroboration, but I believe it is."

Fasi did not respond. He swiveled his chair to face the wall, crossed his legs, and leaned back, resting his head on the back of the chair. He seemed to be in deep thought.

"But, Joe," Scott continued, "even if the jury doesn't buy the perjury, we still have him on two counts of influencing witnesses—five years on each count, with a one-year minimum. Sure, I want to nail Gordon on the subornation charge, but a conviction on any of these charges will surely put him away for years and out of the legal profession forever. Isn't that what we want to accomplish?"

Fasi still did not respond. He sat silently, still turned, facing the wall. Finally he turned toward Scott.

"You are right, Scott. This is going to be a tough one—I'm afraid even tougher than you realize. But you appear to be on the right track, and I'm still going to have you run with it as lead counsel. Let me know when you need help—and keep me posted."

"Of course. I will," Scott said, as he stood to leave. When he reached the door, he paused, and turned. "And thanks, Joe. I really look forward to trying this case. I won't disappoint."

Chapter Eleven

Wednesday, July 30

It was 5:30 p.m., and Scott was sitting at the Library Bar nursing a draft and discussing with Juri their favorite subject, baseball. He was to meet Jennifer there after she finished her research work at the law library. It would be their last night together for several weeks. Jennifer was leaving for Hilton Head in the morning to prepare for her two-week vacation to Europe with her parents. They would be leaving Saturday. Jennifer was trying to wrap up the research for her ARP, which she hoped to complete by mid-September, well in advance of the due date. Today would be a busy one, and she had warned Scott that she might be running late.

It was a slow day behind the bar, so Juri had time to give Scott one of his mini-lectures about the Braves. Forever the pessimist, Juri was sure the Braves were finished for the season.

"Three in a row, Scott. Count 'em—three losses in a row. Eight games behind the lousy Mets. And we're in the weakest division in the majors. Did you see the game last night? Got beat by five runs! And Monday? Got beat by nine. We haven't won a game since last Friday, and that was a sorry-ass Philly team. We're done, Scott, finished!"

"Ah, come on, Juri, you give up too soon. You're talking about the Braves—division titles fourteen consecutive times. You seem to forget that."

"That ended three years ago, Scott. We need Ted Turner to buy the team again. He would put some money in that team. We need a couple more like Chipper Jones. Bobby Cox is the best manager in the game. He could coach a team to the World Series if the owners would just spring for a couple players. Right now we've got one player hitting over three hundred, and that's Chipper. What do you think, Scott?"

Scott was looking toward the entrance and saw Jennifer. "What do I think? I think I see the most beautiful girl in the world coming my way." Scott stood up and turned a swivel barstool around for Jennifer to join him at the bar. Scott took Jennifer's briefcase and placed it at the foot of his bar stool. Then he gently held her hands in both of his and briefly kissed her on the lips.

By the time Jennifer was seated, Juri had her favorite drink ready. He placed it in front of her, and said, "Scott says you're leaving for a couple of weeks, so this one is on me—a going-away present. Which reminds me of a story. You ready?"

Jennifer knew he was going to tell his "story" whether she was "ready" or not. And she knew his "story" would be a blonde joke. He never missed an opportunity. So she just smiled and nodded her head. Scott was smiling also; he knew a blonde joke was inevitable.

Juri already had a broad grin on his face as he began. "The blonde suspects her boyfriend is cheating on her, so she goes out and buys a gun. Then she goes to his apartment. The door's unlocked, and she walks in and finds him in the arms of a beautiful redhead. Well, the blonde is really hurt and angry. Opens her purse and takes out the gun. But she's overcome with grief and puts the gun to her head, finger on the trigger. The boyfriend yells, 'No, honey, don't . . . don't do it!'" Juri stopped and took a deep breath, and his grin turned into a broad smile. "Blonde replies, 'Shut up, you're next!'"

Juri laughed and looked from Scott to Jennifer and back again, waiting for their approval. But he got their usual hisses, boos, and thumbs down. Still, they couldn't help but smile and eventually laugh.

When the laughter subsided, Juri asked Jennifer about her trip. This surprised Scott, who was expecting Juri to begin immediately with his story about the lady lawyer entering the bar with a duck.

"My parents are taking me to Europe for a couple of weeks—early Christmas present. I've never been, but they have. Twice. I don't know the daily schedule, but we have a direct flight from Atlanta to Paris. We'll spend a few days there, and then go visit Normandy—some of the battlefield sites and the American cemetery. My dad's dad—my grandfather—was part of the Normandy invasion. He always claimed he was one of the very lucky ones. He was just twenty years old when he landed on Omaha Beach on D-Day—but he survived that and the rest of the war OK, so I guess he really was one of the lucky ones. We'll also visit the Loire Valley region and some wineries near Bordeaux. My mother wants to visit Copenhagen, so we fly from Paris for a couple of days in Copenhagen at the end of the trip. Maybe too much packed into such a short time, but I'm really looking forward to it. I get back just a few days before the start of the fall semester. And, Juri, I want you to watch out for Scott while I'm gone. Keep him busy and out of trouble."

"Sure, Jennifer," Juri said. "Keeping Scott busy won't be a problem. He's got that big case he's working on—the Harrison case . . . no, I mean Harrison's attorney, that Max guy. Right, Scott?"

And as was often the case with Juri, he did not wait for a response before continuing. "And maybe we can work in a trip to Atlanta for a game. The Braves are at the Diamondbacks next weekend, but the following weekend they are home for a three-day stand with the Giants. How about it, Scott? We can zip up in your Camaro in three hours, maybe less."

"I have an automobile, Juri, not an airplane. But you get us some good seats, right behind home plate, and we'll do it." Scott was amazed at how Juri kept the complete schedule of the Atlanta Braves in his head.

"I'll get 'em. And I'll take care of him, Jennifer." Juri stopped and smiled. "Two weeks, eh? I know Scott's got more on his mind than baseball, so you guys get out of here. I've got the tab."

Chapter Twelve

Thursday, August 7

Joe Fasi was in his office examining the new felony cases. One of his duties was to assign the new cases to the assistant DAs in the Felony Division. It was a time-consuming job, important but unappealing. It seemed that lately there were always more cases coming in than being disposed. Every assistant was carrying much more than Fasi felt reasonable, but there was no easy solution. In fact, there was no *real solution*—easy or otherwise. But it had to be done. Dividing cases evenly to each assistant did not work. Some cases took much more time than others, such as capital cases, child victim cases, and gang-related cases. Young and inexperienced prosecutors often took twice as much time to bring a case to disposition as experienced prosecutors. And many of his assistants had less than five years' experience. Then there were those cases that appeared rather simple at first look but became quite complex upon further investigation, or when special defenses, such as insanity, were claimed. And all of this was compounded when a private attorney, whose fee was usually based on the amount of trial preparation and length of trial, entered the case, causing more delays and court appearances. Fasi not only had to assign the cases as they came in but monitor the ongoing case load of each assistant. This supervisory work took him out of the place he loved—the courtroom—except for a few exceptional cases that he assigned to himself as lead prosecutor, or second chair as in the Gordon case.

Shortly before 9:00 a.m., Fasi's phone rang. It was Janna O'Meara, secretary for Joshua Magidson, the district attorney.

"Mr. Magidson wants to see you right away, like now," Janna said.

"I'll be right up," Fasi replied. This was important, he knew, from the "like now." The DA usually scheduled an appointment.

When Fasi arrived at the DA's office, he found Detective John Majewski of the Savannah-Chatham Metropolitan Police Department, seated in one of the chairs near the DA's desk.

"Joe, I believe you know Detective John Majewski," Magidson said, extending his hand in the direction of Majewski.

"Of course; we've worked a number of cases together," Fasi responded.

"Have a seat. John wants to brief us on an incident that occurred last night. He informed me briefly of the subject, so I sent for you to hear the details. It involves a serious personnel matter." Magidson then turned to Majewski with a worried look on his face. "So, let's hear the details."

Majewski was a 28-year-veteran police officer, tall and fit, with a full head of salt and pepper hair. His clean-shaven face had a perpetual severe look on it, but Fasi had always found him cordial and professional, as well as an unflappable witness. His memory of investigations over the years was legend. He could recall like yesterday people and events that he had investigated years ago. He was the go-to detective when other detectives needed advice in difficult or high-profile cases. He carried himself like a drill sergeant, ramrod straight when walking and ramrod straight when sitting, as now.

"Even though the investigation is still ongoing, we knew you would want an initial report right away. We aren't certain of the specific charges as of now, but the facts appear clear. It occurred at the Henry Grady Inn, on Drayton Street. Are you familiar with that inn?" Majewski looked at Fasi as he spoke.

"No, I'm not," Fasi said. "I've seen it in passing, but that's all I know about it."

"And I'm not familiar with it either," added Magidson.

Majewski continued. "It's a bed and breakfast, two stories, Victorian style with a large, open, wraparound front porch. It's on the east side of Drayton Street, about forty feet from the sidewalk. Drayton as you know, is one-way and runs south to north. There is a bus stop in front, with a wooden bench. About eleven-fifteen last night, a young lady—Monica Ashley, a tourist from Atlanta—stepped outside to smoke. Smoking is not allowed inside or on the porch, so she walked down the steps to the sidewalk and took a seat on the bench by the bus stop. She had a cell phone with her—an iPhone, the new one just released in June. The area there is well-lit from nearby street lights and lights from the porch and yard of the inn, so she felt safe. She saw a car moving slowly north on Drayton, close to the curb. It didn't stop, but in a couple of minutes, it came by again, and this time stopped in front of the bench where the young lady was seated. A young white man was driving—the only person she saw in the vehicle. He rolled down his window on the passenger side and called out something she didn't understand. Ms. Ashley thought he could be lost and asking directions, so she wasn't too concerned. She just yelled back something like, 'I'm not from here, don't know the streets.' She's not sure exactly what she said, but she wasn't frightened."

Majewski pulled out a photo from his briefcase, and passed it to Magidson.

"Here's a photo of the inn, taken by a police photographer. You can see the bench and the steps that lead up to the inn. The spot where the photographer was standing when he took the photo would be about where the vehicle stopped."

Magidson looked at the photo for a moment, then passed it to Fasi.

Majewski began again. "Then the man got out of his vehicle, walked behind it and approached the lady, who had just lit her cigarette. She remained seated, as he did not appear to be threatening. The man stopped five or six feet from her, and said, 'Let's go party.' She did not get it immediately, but then he said, 'I've got cash. Let's go.' That's when she realized he believed she was a prostitute. She shouted, 'Get away. Get away!' She was still seated, and he grabbed her by the right arm and tried to pull her into the vehicle. She screamed and struggled, broke his grip, but fell on the sidewalk. He quickly went back around to the driver's door, got in, and left the scene. Would have been all we had, except for this."

Majewski pulled another photo from his briefcase and passed it to the district attorney.

"Fortunately, she wasn't hurt, and she kept her senses throughout the ordeal. As soon as she saw the guy running to the driver's side of the vehicle, she got her phone, which had been beside her on the bench, and snapped a photo. As you see, it's a clear photo of the right rear of the vehicle, including the license plate, Georgia—GRE1345."

Magidson looked at the photo for a long moment before passing it to Fasi. Fasi studied it as Majewski continued.

"As soon as she snapped the photo, she called 911. A precinct patrolman came within minutes, joined by another very shortly. We didn't have a detective readily available at the time and since she was safe and there were no injuries, they took her statement and some photos. She gave the patrolman her iPhone, and he pulled up the photo with the license plate number. They ran the number and found the owner. Then they pulled up the owner's driver's license on a computer in a patrol vehicle and asked her if he was the man who attacked her. She said she thought he was—not the way we would like to have an ID, but that's what we have. Early this morning one of our precinct detectives went to the inn to follow up on the investigation begun by the patrol officers last night, but the lady had already checked out. We have her Atlanta address and phone number, but really regret we weren't able to get a better ID and a more complete investigation this morning before she left. There was also one other witness. He's the night manager at the inn, a graduate student at Savannah State. He was in the vestibule of the inn when he heard the scream. He ran outside in time to see the vehicle pulling away from the curb, but he didn't see the driver and couldn't make an ID. He did identify the automobile in the photo as the one he saw pulling away as he ran outside. We'll be interviewing him again."

Magidson interrupted. "Joe, I know you are wondering why I asked you to come in on this. The reason is that it involves one of our assistants. I asked Detective Majewski not to mention the name before he briefed you because I wanted you to hear the facts first. Personally, I was a bit shocked. And I knew you would be also because of your relationship with the alleged attacker. Go ahead, John."

"The automobile is a Camaro Z28, registered to Scott Marino. And he was identified by the lady from the driver's license photo."

Fasi had been leaning forward in his chair as he listened to the report, but with Majewski's revelation, he pushed back, stunned and speechless. Finally, as if to himself, he said, "That's so unbelievable. Never in a . . ." He stopped and turned away, visibly shaken.

"Well, we'll just have to deal with it," Magidson said. "What's next for this investigation, John?"

"We want to have the lady make a better ID with a good photo array. We'll probably have to go to Atlanta to do that. She was adamant in saying she had a busy work schedule and would not be able to return to Savannah soon. We want to get that photo ID as soon as possible, so we'll go to her. Do you have a photo of Marino that we can have?"

"Yes, there will be one in his personnel file." Magidson reached for his phone. "Janna, would you step in here now with Scott Marino's personnel file?" His secretary entered with the file, and the photo was handed to Majewski.

"Will you be going to Atlanta for the photo lineup?" asked Magidson.

"Not sure it will be me, but probably," said Majewski.

Fasi finally spoke, his face stressed. He took a deep breath before he began. His speech was slow and very soft. "Have you considered the possibility that the vehicle was stolen? She only got a brief view of the driver, and her ID was not very positive."

Majewski pulled another photo from his file. "About four this morning, the precinct patrolman went to the apartment address of the registered vehicle owner. There he found the vehicle in the parking lot of the address, and he took a photo." Majewski handed the photo to Fasi. It was a similar view as the other photo, showing the right rear of the Z28, the license plate, and right rear tire.

"And you can see," Majewski continued, "same license plate, same vehicle. And though you can't see it in the photo, the patrolman noted something else. The steering wheel had a locking device on it—'The Club.' Not unusual for an owner of that kind of automobile—no one was going to ever get a chance to steal his vehicle. No, we aren't dealing with the driver of a stolen vehicle."

Fasi handed the photo to Magidson, who looked at it briefly and then said, "You know, John, when you finally send the investigation to us, we'll have to recuse our office from prosecuting the case. I'll request another DA's office to come in for the prosecution. And it may be a good idea for your office to call in the GBI and do likewise. You and most of those in your office worked the Harrison cases with this young prosecutor. You personally know him, and maybe along with others in the Metro Police Department have developed a friendship. Could cause some distraction in the investigation."

Majewski nodded his head in agreement. "Yes, could do that. I'll take it up with Major Bodiford."

"Anything else we should know now, John?" asked Magidson.

"No, that's about it. We can probably wrap it up pretty soon after we get a better ID with the photo lineup. We won't be questioning Mr. Marino until we get the photo ID. And please don't make Mr. Marino aware of our investigation until we question him."

"Only Joe and I know of it, and we'll keep it that way," Magidson replied. "I'm sure you'll keep us apprised as you proceed with the investigation. Let me know if my office can help."

Magidson stood, indicating the briefing was over. He walked from behind his desk and shook Majewski's hand. Then he said, "John, I'm sure you will keep all of this absolutely in-house, need-to-know only, until the investigation is complete and received here. That's very important. Scott Marino is involved in prosecuting a high-profile case—the Max Gordon case—as well as other felony cases. We are going to have to make a number of in-house adjustments, and I prefer to do that before this incident becomes known and widespread."

"Certainly. I'll be overseeing it and can do that. And if the GBI gets involved, I'll make sure they understand also."

As Majewski left the room, Magidson turned to Fasi. "Now," he said, "let's discuss those adjustments."

Chapter Thirteen

Fasi had remained seated as Majewski left. As soon as the door was shut, he asked, "Mind if I take a couple minutes before we discuss those adjustments?"

"Not at all. I think we both need a break to let this all sink in."

Fasi rose from his chair, walked slowly to the window, folded his arms and looked down on Montgomery Street, six stories below. There had been an early morning rain, but the sun was now out with a promise of another beautiful but hot summer day in Savannah. He stood there gazing at the flame rising from the "Flame of Freedom" monument at the front entrance and watching men and women scurrying in and out of the courthouse. He was just watching, not thinking. It was midmorning, and he already felt tired, as if it had been a long trial day. He took a deep breath and returned to sit in his chair across from his boss.

"This is a tough blow to me personally, Josh. I really respected that young man," Fasi said. "And a tough blow to our Felony Division. Scott is one of the hardest working assistants I've ever witnessed. Only a couple of years here, but his energy and intelligence made up for his lack of experience. I had high expectations for him—he's a natural in the courtroom. For some time now all the felony prosecutors have been carrying a very heavy load, and he's carrying one of the heaviest. Besides the Gordon case, he's got a full load of active and serious felonies. It's not going to be easy replacing him."

"We can agree on that, but it has to be done. I want you to relieve him immediately of the Gordon case. When this assault hits the newspapers, our whole office—right or wrong—will be a big part of the news, and I don't want to read that the prosecutor for the Gordon case has been arrested. Max Gordon is not going down easily, and he would find some way to work it into the trial. And don't assign Scott any more cases. Let him keep what he has for now, at least until we hear more on the investigation. Any questions?"

Fasi wasn't pleased with the district attorney's "adjustments," yet he realized they were reasonable, and he couldn't think of any better solution. Sure, he had questions, but he realized the answers would have to come from himself.

"No questions," he replied.

Fasi left the DA's office to take an action he dreaded. He preferred to wait until sometime in midafternoon, but the district attorney had used the word "immediately." He hoped he would catch Scott in his office. He phoned and Scott answered.

"Scott, I need to see you right away. Can you come to my office now?"

"Sure, I'll be right down."

When Scott arrived, Fasi motioned for him to take a seat. This would be unpleasant, but he would get it done—now.

"Scott, I just had a discussion with the DA. I'm going to be taking over the lead in the Gordon case, at his specific request. You will be devoting all your time to the other cases assigned to you but will have no further responsibility or assignment in the Gordon case. I don't have a full answer for the reason or reasons right now—maybe later. Just consider it done. Send me the file with all the work you've done on it. I know that's considerable. I realize this may be a disappointment, but the upside is you'll have more time for all your other cases."

Scott rose from his chair and stood facing Fasi with a perplexed look on his face. "So I'm fired and no explanation?"

"Let's say relieved. I hope we'll get an explanation, but right now that's not important. What is important is that I get up to date with that case right away, so make sure you get the file to me this afternoon."

Still standing, Scott extended both hands, palms up, toward Fasi. "Joe, do you really think this is fair? Just relieve me, no reason given?"

"Probably not, Scott. I don't like passing the buck to someone else, but really, it's not my call. I hope there will be a satisfactory explanation coming."

"I'll have the file and all related papers on your desk sometime this afternoon," Scott said, as he turned and walked out the door.

Driving home that afternoon, Fasi could not get the day's stunning events out of his mind. He wondered if it was pressure from the heavy workload that caused such aberrant behavior in Scott. *Had he missed signs that he should have noted?* He knew Scott was usually in the office, deep into his work, before most others even arrived. *Should he have insisted that Scott take more time off? Or lightened his load?* And he wondered what the final charges would be. It was pretty clear that several misdemeanor crimes could be charged—disorderly conduct, assault and battery, pandering, and soliciting sex, if they wanted to pile it on. But he was sure the investigators would look for a more serious crime, a felony, such as attempted kidnapping. But he knew it really made no difference as far as Scott's career as an assistant district attorney was concerned. Considering the circumstances, even just one of the minor charges would result in his firing. A more serious charge would affect Scott more than the office, but the office would be affected either way.

Fasi was driving south on Whitaker Street. When he reached Forsyth Park, he found a parking spot, got out of his car, and walked slowly into the park. The sun was beginning to set, and the park was unusually quiet. He stopped briefly at the fountain and then walked into the wooded area on the north end of the park. Dark shadows from the towering oaks surrounded him. He found an isolated bench and sat there until the sun was completely down. His mind kept turning over the day's events. He was not happy with how he dismissed Scott from the Gordon case. It was cold, seemingly uncaring. If he had not been required to do it immediately, maybe they could have gone for a beer after work. But it still would not have been easy. He really respected this young man. He had found him to be a smart, quick learner. He had watched him closely in the Harrison murder trial and observed his natural trial skills. He liked his character, his work habits, his ethics—perhaps seeing a lot of himself in him.

His thoughts drifted back to that morning in the DA's office when he learned of the investigation. *Why had he and the DA accepted so quickly the report of Majewski? It was all based on reports of others. Majewski had no personal knowledge. The investigation was still ongoing. And Scott was given no opportunity to explain or deny before he was relieved.*

He sat there quietly, as darkness enveloped him. And he had no answers.

Chapter Fourteen

Friday, August 8

After his briefing of the district attorney on Thursday, Majewski met with Major Joe Bodiford, Chief of Criminal Investigations for the Savannah-Chatham Metropolitan Police Department, to discuss whether they should invite the Georgia Bureau of Investigation to assist. It was true, as noted by the district attorney, that many of the Metro detectives had worked with Scott, and some would be considered friends. None would take delight in presenting the charges that this investigation would likely produce. Besides, the department was already stretched thin by the cases now being investigated—never enough time and never enough investigators. Bodiford decided to request assistance from the GBI. He made the phone call and set up a meeting for Majewski and Special Agent Carl DeBickero of the Georgia Bureau of Investigation for Friday afternoon in Majewski's office.

Carl worked out of the Region 5 GBI Office in Statesboro. Savannah was within his region's jurisdiction, so he was in Savannah frequently. Majewski was pleased that Carl would be involved. They were longtime friends and had worked many cases together over the years. But it was more than friendship. Carl was one of the most experienced and respected investigators in the bureau. He had investigated about every crime in the book and a few that weren't. Majewski had called on him several times when he had hit a dead end, and usually Carl was able to suggest a way to restart it.

When Carl arrived, they took five or six minutes to catch up before Majewski began to brief him on the investigation. As soon as Scott Marino's name was mentioned as the suspect, Carl held up his hand.

"You mean Scott Marino, the assistant DA?" Carl asked incredulously.

"Yes, prosecutor in the Harrison trials," said Majewski.

Carl's eyes narrowed before replying. "Can't be. Really can't be." He emphasized every word. "No way can I believe that. I investigated the Nolan case in Effingham County. Remember that one?"

Majewski paused for a moment as he thought. "That was the law professor who abducted one of his students and held her captive?"

"Right. That was where I first met Marino. He was responsible for her rescue. And I'm the lead investigator in the Gordon case. Marino has been my main contact. Been working with him closely for months. He's a straight shooter. No way he would be involved. You've got the wrong guy, Mo."

"Sorry, I should have remembered your connection. Just didn't think about it. Wouldn't have had you come in. We requested GBI assistance because so many here have been involved in his cases. And many of us know him personally. You probably have the same concern. You want to hear more about it, or do you think you can't get involved because of your working relationship?" asked Majewski.

"Well, I'm already here. Let me hear what you have, and I'll decide whether I can participate."

Majewski gave Carl essentially the same briefing he had given Fasi and the district attorney on Thursday. Carl listened carefully, shaking his head frequently in disbelief.

"That's about it," Majewski finally said, placing the photos back in the folder and closing it.

Carl paused only a moment before responding. "No questions on the investigation. With the photos and eyewitnesses, it looks solid. But you asked if I thought I could get involved, considering my personal knowledge of Marino. Well, I have no problem assisting, even taking the lead. It is what it is. I've handled many investigations where I hoped the target would be exonerated. Some have, some haven't. I just follow the evidence. I'll do it in this case. From what you've shown me, I already have a pretty good idea where the evidence will lead. But it's still open and you suggest the next step should be a photo ID by the victim—and soon. Count me in. I'll do it this weekend. Let me have your folder, whatever you have so far."

Majewski handed Carl the folder. Carl opened it and removed some papers. "I'm looking for a phone number and address," he said. He examined the papers. "I've got it. I see a note by the phone number that says it's her brother's."

"Yes, that's because the only phone she had was her cell phone, and we are keeping that for a while as part of the investigation." Majewski opened his desk drawer, pulled out a cell phone and handed it to Carl. "Here's her phone. She wasn't at all happy about our keeping it. The precinct patrolman who took it promised to get it back to her as soon as possible, but we need to hold on to it until the investigation is complete."

Majewski and Carl sat and talked for several more minutes, during which Majewski gave the file to a secretary to make a copy of everything in it. It was agreed that the investigation would be taken over by the GBI, with Savannah detectives assisting as needed. Carl would conduct the photo lineup that weekend in Atlanta. After the photo lineup, Marino would be interviewed by a Metro detective with no previous work or personal relationship with him. It was understood that the investigation would be given priority for earliest completion and that all involved in the investigation would be informed that it was to be kept confidential until completion.

"I'll let you know the result of the photo lineup no later than Monday," Carl said, as he was leaving.

Chapter Fifteen

Saturday, August 9

Special Agent DeBickero drove to Atlanta Saturday morning with his wife, Karen. Karen's mother lived in Atlanta. They had planned the trip several days before the meeting with Majewski on Friday. It may have been one of the reasons he agreed to conduct the photo lineup with the witness. It would not involve a special trip, making it convenient for all involved.

But that was not the major reason he agreed to take over the investigation. It was because Scott Marino was the prime suspect in this crime. He knew this young man, and he could not imagine him capable of committing the act that Majewski had described. Carl believed himself to be a good judge of character and wanted in on the investigation so that he could be assured of the truth. He knew he was leaving himself open for criticism because of his past relationship with Marino, but he could handle it. He took the lead in the investigation not to exonerate Marino but to get to the absolute truth. If the facts led to Marino as the assailant, he would personally arrest him and see that he was brought swiftly to justice.

They arrived in Atlanta shortly before 1:00 p.m. and had lunch with Karen's mother. Afterwards, he used his cell phone to call the number he had for Monica Ashley. Aware that this was her brother's number, he was not surprised by the male voice that answered.

"This is Carl DeBickero. I'm a special agent for the Georgia Bureau of Investigation. I'd like to speak with Monica Ashley if she is available."

"Tell me why you're calling," came the response.

"I'm following up on the incident she reported when she was in Savannah last Wednesday night."

There was a long pause. "Well, she's not here."

"When do you expect her?"

"I don't expect her."

"What do you mean?"

"I mean I don't expect her."

It appeared to Carl that the man, perhaps her brother, was trying to be a smart-ass, but he would be patient.

"Can you tell me how I may get in touch with her? She gave us this number as the phone to call to contact her. It's important that I speak with her."

There was another long pause. "If you want to leave your phone number, I can give it to her when I see her. If I see her."

"Isn't this her brother's phone number?"

The man laughed into the phone. "Listen, if you want to give me your phone number, like I said, I'll tell her you want her to call when I see her. That's all I can do."

Carl gave the man his cell phone number, again emphasizing that it was important that she call. He wondered about the notation that it was her brother's phone number. He suspected that he would not receive a call from Monica Ashley anytime soon.

But he had her address, apparently an apartment—925B Peachtree Street NE. He had hoped to save time by making a phone call, but since that was unsuccessful, he would just drive over to her apartment. It was 4:30 p.m., and he realized that a young lady living in Atlanta was likely to have plans for a Saturday evening. He hoped to catch her before she left. He put the address in his GPS. It appeared to be about a twenty-minute drive.

As he approached the address, he was surprised to find that it was in a very busy commercial district. And when he arrived, he saw it was a UPS Store. He found a parking spot and walked to the store. A sign on the door listed the hours of operation for Saturday as 10:00 a.m. to 3:00 p.m. It was closed for business, but the doors were open, making the mailboxes accessible. Monica could receive her mail anytime day or night—she was always "home" for the mailman but not for a GBI agent looking for her. As he walked back to his car, he thought about the situation. *This simple photo lineup assignment was getting to be a real pain in the backside.*

Chapter Sixteen

Sunday, August 10

Carl spent much of Sunday morning going over the details in the investigative report that he had received from Majewski. He compared the photos of the rear of the vehicle. He noted the good camera work. Each photo was very clear, taken with steady hands, no movement distortion. He would expect that for the photo taken by the patrolman, but he was surprised that someone who had just been assaulted could hold a camera so steady. Then he examined the cell phone to see if it contained any other photos, saved calls, text messages, or other information that may help with his efforts to locate Monica Ashley. He was surprised that it was so clean. Almost no third-party apps and just a few photos, all of Savannah scenes. There were no text messages and just a couple of outgoing calls. He had hoped to find a large phone log that would be helpful in locating Monica if the phone number he had did not pan out.

Carl called the number at 2:00 p.m. Sunday afternoon and again asked to speak to Monica Ashley.

The same voice answered. "Listen, buddy, I told you yesterday she wasn't here. I take messages. I relay messages. I don't return messages. Got it?"

Not what he had hoped to hear, but he knew he must keep his cool if he was to make progress. "Would you mind telling me what you can about Monica Ashley? Apparently you know her. I have her new cell phone and I want to return it."

"Know her?" The man laughed. "Can't say. But I'll let her know that you have her cell phone."

"Then apparently you know how to contact her. So why don't you just tell me how I can contact her—save you the trouble."

"Now wouldn't that be nice," the man responded. Then he heard him hang up.

Yes, that would be nice, you asshole, Carl said to himself. He suddenly realized that locating Monica Ashley was going to take more effort than a phone call—or a drive over to a UPS store. But he would find her. He thought of calling one of his Atlanta detective contacts, but Sunday afternoon did not seem to be the time to call in a favor. There was no emergency here. Monday would be soon enough.

Chapter Seventeen

Monday, August 11

Monday morning Carl called a friend, Frank Edwards, of the Atlanta Police Department Criminal Investigation Division. Edwards and Carl had worked closely on several cases, including the Gordon case. Edwards was part of the joint federal-state task force that broke the drug syndicate leading to Clarence Wilborn's arrest. Afterwards, he was instrumental in getting Wilborn to turn on Gordon for a plea that would give Wilborn a much milder sentence. Edwards made sure that Wilborn understood that he could receive the maximum—twenty years to life—if he didn't cooperate. Carl was sure the perjury investigation would never have been solved without Wilborn's arrest and Edwards' help.

Over the phone, Carl explained his unproductive Saturday and Sunday phone conversations.

"Sounds like an 'exchange' number," Edwards said.

Carl was familiar with the term, though it had never been a factor in any of his investigations.

"Give me a few minutes to check it out. But that's the way some prostitutes market themselves. Had you not identified yourself with the GBI, you would probably have gotten that return call, and you could have discussed where, what, and how much. With an 'exchange number,' both the hooker and the john are protected. *She* doesn't have to be a sidewalk hostess, and *he* can wait in private for her phone call. The john can call for a particular prostitute, or just something off the rack. And the phone exchange system allows the pimp better control. A sleazy business, but we've got a lot of it here in Atlanta."

"Atlanta and everywhere else," Carl replied. "Tough racket to control. Give me a call when you confirm that this is an exchange number."

Twenty minutes later, Edwards called. "Yes, it's an exchange. You can probably set up a meeting by calling again, but Carl, probably not a good idea to announce you work for the GBI." They both laughed.

"And I can't use my own cell phone again," said Carl. "I'll use the room phone. But I'm pretty sure my wife's not going to be happy with me renting a cheap motel room to meet a hooker. You have a better idea, Frank?"

"No, and I think that's what you'll have to do if you want to have that photo lineup. But do you suppose the switchboard guy will recognize your voice when you call?"

"Not a chance. I've got several voices that I've used in this business. Got one straight from the Bronx. *Whadda ya tawkin' aboud? I went to foist grade in Lawn Guyland. Yooz tinks I'm stoopid?*"

They laughed. "Any suggestions for a motel where I can set this up?" DeBickero asked. "No five-star place—I'll have to justify this expense. But something comfortable—I may have to wait a while."

"Yes, there's a perfect place—Palomino Motel on Parkway Drive Northeast. It has a horsehead sign out front, big lighted sign—maybe eight by ten. You would think it would picture a palomino, but it's a light bay with a black mane. Looks like a sign painter mistake, but I suspect it's deliberate—makes people remember the place. I did some undercover work there when we were investigating the drug syndicate that Wilborn was involved in. Should be able to get a room for about a hundred—not fancy, but clean and comfortable."

They spoke for a few more minutes, with Edwards providing an update on the drug syndicate cases. Carl said he would call him on Tuesday with an update of his Palomino Motel results, and they hung up.

Shortly after his conversation with Edwards, Carl called Majewski in Savannah, detailing the unsuccessful search for Monica Ashley.

"So, bottom line, I don't know when I'll make contact."

"We were hoping to have that photo lineup completed before we interview Marino. Maybe we should go ahead with it anyway," Majewski said.

"Yeah, I think so. Depending on what he says—or admits—could change the course of the investigation. I'm not happy waiting in a motel room for some call girl to come calling. And I don't plan to spend the night in that motel. If I don't get a return call from Monica by ten tonight, I'll be gone."

"OK, we'll interview Marino ASAP."

"Call me with the results," said Carl. "Like I said, it could impact what I'm doing here in Atlanta."

Chapter Eighteen

Monday, August 11

Carl checked in at the Palomino Motel in midafternoon—room 207 on the second floor, next to the elevator. The furnishings were simple but adequate, typical of motels in that price range. There was a queen-size bed with bedside table and phone, lounge chair, dresser with 32" TV on top, desk with lamp and wooden chair, and a small bathroom. He placed his briefcase containing the investigative file on the bed and made his call to the "exchange."

The male voice that answered did not sound like the voice he heard the last two times he had called, but he used his Bronx accent anyway. All went as expected. He left the motel's address, phone number, his room number, and first name.

He turned on the TV, then sat in the lounge chair to wait for a call from Monica. He clicked through the TV listings. Nothing much interested him. He would just watch CNN until Monday Night Football came on at 8:00 p.m. He was a Green Bay Packers fan, and they would be playing the Bengals. The Braves would not be playing, having just finished a four-game series with the Arizona Diamondbacks—and losing three out of the four.

He had been watching CNN for about forty-five minutes when the phone rang. He picked it up quickly.

"Hello."

"Is this Carl?"

"It is. Monica?"

"Yes. Would you like me to come over now?"

"Yes, how soon can you be here?"

"Twenty, twenty-five minutes. Is this an all-nighter?"

Carl was feeling his way with this conversation. He had never been involved in a prostitution sting operation, even when starting out with the Richmond County Sheriff's Department in Augusta, Georgia, many years ago. His investigative duties with the GBI did not involve prostitution rings, though prostitutes were occasionally the victims of homicides he investigated. He wasn't sure what the best answer to this question should be. But he had to answer, and quickly.

"No, I'll probably check out tonight."

"Then let's plan on an hour. How does two-fifty sound?"

Two hundred fifty dollars sounded pretty high to Carl, but he was sure she didn't mean two dollars and fifty cents. He had no idea of the going rate. He took a chance. "Seems a bit high, that the best I can get?"

"Honey, you gonna get the best. But, Carl, you sound nice. Two hundred, cash—for you. OK?"

"OK, cash. I'll be here."

The knock on his door came thirty minutes later. He opened it to find a woman, perhaps in her mid-thirties, smiling, and holding a small handbag. She was dressed in low-rise denim shorts and a white, sleeveless crop top exposing four or five inches of a flat and tanned abdomen. Her dark hair had been pulled back in a tight pony tail. Her makeup was a bit overstated, but someone about to pay for a quick romp in a motel room would likely find her reasonably attractive.

"I'm Monica. May I come in, Carl?"

Carl replied, "Of course," and stepped aside.

Monica walked over by the dresser, leaned on it slightly, and said, "Carl, do you have something for me? I have something for you." She smiled and held out her hand, palm up.

Carl handed her ten twenty-dollar bills, which Monica quickly counted and placed in her handbag. She then began to remove her top.

"Don't bother," said Carl, as he reached in his front pocket, removed his GBI badge, and displayed it to Monica.

Monica stared at it, her eyes wide, the smile quickly gone. Then she took two deep but quick breaths and nervously asked, "Am I being arrested?"

"Not yet and maybe we can avoid it. First, remove the bills I just handed you, place them on the bed and take a seat in that chair in front of the desk."

Monica reached for her handbag and quickly complied. Her eyes tightened, and she was clenching her jaw. Carl was sure this was not her first encounter with law enforcement, but still, she appeared quite frightened.

Carl remained standing. "I didn't ask you here to set you up for a prostitution arrest. I can and will if it becomes necessary. But if you answer my questions truthfully, you can walk out of here freely, without any consequences. Understand?"

Monica responded with an affirmative nod of her head.

"First, I want your real name. Monica is not your real name, is it?"

Again, Monica did not say anything but responded with a negative shake of her head.

"Let me see your driver's license."

Monica reached into her handbag and took out a wallet. The driver's license was in a window of the wallet. She offered the wallet to Carl.

"No, I don't want the wallet. Just remove the driver's license."

When Carl received the license, he looked at the photo and made some notes in the file. He noted her date of birth. She was now twenty-six years old but looked much older. Her profession was really taking a toll.

"So, your name is Glenna Norris, is that right?"

"Yes."

"Glenna, I'm here to follow up on the incident in which you were assaulted in Savannah last week. I want you to tell me everything you can recall."

Carl was trying not to look severely at Glenna as he spoke. She was already frightened. He needed her to relax a bit so that she could relate her story fully. Hoping to calm her, he took a seat across from her and spoke in a softened voice.

"Now, I want you to start at the beginning. I need all the details you can recall. It's important that we get all the information so that we can successfully prosecute the person responsible for the assault."

"I just . . . I just can't remember much now. I had been drinking that night, and it happened so quick. I just can't bring anything to mind."

Carl was surprised at this statement. There was nothing, not a hint, in the investigative report that the victim had been drinking and certainly nothing to indicate she was drunk. In fact, she had identified the driver from his Georgia driver's license photo, shown on the screen of the computer in the patrol car.

Carl removed an 8"x10" print of the picture she had taken with her camera immediately after the assault.

"Glenna, do you recall taking this photo?"

"I don't know. I guess so."

"I'm not asking if you recall the numbers on the license plate. I'm just asking if you recognize the photo. We printed it from your camera."

"I just. . . I . . . I just can't be sure."

"Glenna, if I were to show you a photo of the individual who attacked you, do you think you would recognize him?"

"I don't think so."

This was making no sense. She had already made an ID, but the manner in which it was made—displaying a single facial photo from a driver's license—was insufficient. Carl had an array of photos, all the same race and approximate age of Marino. He was here to make a proper ID, but now the victim said she didn't believe she would recognize him. Not a good start, but he would display them anyway. It might jog her memory. He reached into his briefcase and removed the photos. He spread six photos lengthwise on the bed. Marino's photo was not among them.

"Glenna, I want you to look at these six photos. The man that attacked you may or may not be among them. Take a close look. Do you see the man who attacked you in any of these photos?"

She looked, then said, "No, I don't."

So far, so good. Carl spread another six photos on the bed. This time, Marino's photo was among them. The same instructions were given.

"No, I don't see him," Glenna responded.

Carl picked up all the photos and put them back in his briefcase. He did not believe her. She did not appear to want to cooperate with the investigation.

"Glenna, you understand we are trying to identify the man who assaulted you. You do want to see him prosecuted, don't you?"

"I guess so."

"You guess so? Glenna, how long had you been in Savannah when you were assaulted?"

"Just that day."

"Why were you there?"

"Just to visit, look around."

"How did you get there? Drive or fly?"

"We drove."

"Who is 'we'?"

"Oh, just a guy who drove us down."

"Just the two of you?"

"Yes."

"What is the name of the guy who drove you to Savannah?"

Glenna did not respond. She shrugged, then looked around the room—at the TV, which was now off, at a picture on the far wall, anywhere except at Carl. Carl waited patiently for a response, but Glenna remained silent.

"Glenna, what is the name of the man?" Carl repeated, more forcefully.

Another long pause and another shrug. Then, "I'm not really sure—we had just met. And now I've forgotten."

"Don't recall even his first name?"

Glenna placed both of her palms tightly against her eyes, then removed them and crossed her arms against her chest, hands now firmly clutching the opposite arm. She appeared to shudder. But she did not speak.

"I've explained I'm not here to arrest you. But I may, Glenna, if you refuse to cooperate. I need your assistance. I need you to tell me all that you remember about that trip to Savannah. Do you understand?"

Again, she did not speak, but nodded her head. Then she dropped her chin to her chest and began to breathe heavily.

"Glenna, are you afraid to tell me something?"

She raised her chin and looked at Carl and said, "I just don't remember anything. I just can't remember."

Carl wasn't convinced. He continued the questioning for another half-hour, but the results were the same. She claimed to recall nothing. Sometimes quietly crying, then looking around the room to focus briefly on a picture, the TV, the door—but rarely speaking. She gave no useful information.

Eventually Carl realized that it was highly unlikely any useful information would be forthcoming. She appeared to be frightened, not by him, but by what he was asking her to do: reveal all she knew about the assault in Savannah. Why? He had no idea. He had several choices. One, he could continue this futile questioning. Two, he could call the Atlanta police, explain the meeting and have her arrested for prostitution. But that would not likely help with his investigation. Or three, he could just let her go now, and follow up later. He now had her real name and address and other information that would make locating her easier, and if *he* couldn't locate her, he was sure Frank Edwards could. Maybe the interview with Marino would reveal some information that would change the focus of the investigation. He decided on option three. Besides, he was ready to leave the Palomino Motel for a good night's sleep. He would call Frank Edwards the next day with a report of the meeting so he could keep him in the loop.

Chapter Nineteen

Monday, August 11

While Carl was checking into the Palomino Motel expecting to complete a photo lineup of Scott Marino, Marino was arriving at the office of Detective Michael Kohl of the Savannah Metro Police Special Victims Crime Unit. Kohl had been selected to interview Marino by Majewski because he was an experienced investigator who did not know Marino professionally or socially. Majewski wanted the interview to proceed without any accusations. None of the questions were to alert Marino that he was a suspect in this crime. Majewski knew this type of interview ran counter to the opinion of other experienced detectives, who believed that much could be gained from a direct accusation. In fact, in many cases, it did lead to an immediate confession, or some statement that was eventually incriminating.

But here they were dealing with an attorney experienced in criminal law. A confession was not to be expected. His responses would be limited and studied. So, Majewski instructed, it was to be a wide-open interview—no accusation, just general information such as his knowledge of the Henry Grady Inn, his whereabouts on that night, and if the photos were of his vehicle. Lock him in on as much personal information about that night as he could, and record it all. As soon as he had been notified Monday morning of this assignment, Kohl placed a phone call to Marino and arranged for an interview that afternoon.

He was surprised that Marino did not ask about the purpose of the interview. He spent the rest of the morning at his desk analyzing the investigative report and preparing for the interview. He had never had to question a prosecutor or any other attorney who was a prime suspect. He expected this to be difficult, but he would prepare the best he could.

Scott arrived shortly before 4:00 p.m. Kohl had two arm chairs arranged facing each other, near his desk. On his desk was the investigative file and a small cassette recorder. Scott was directed to one of the chairs and Kohl began the interview.

"Scott, I'm investigating an incident that occurred last Wednesday night. But first, I'd like to get some background information. Do you mind if we record this interview?"

"Not at all. Go ahead."

Kohl spoke to the recorder, giving the date, time, place, and parties present, then asking Scott to spell his last name. Scott did so.

"And I have your permission to record this interview, correct?"

"Sure, no problem."

"Scott, I don't think we've ever met, but I believe you are an assistant district attorney with the Chatham County DA's office, correct?"

"Yes."

"What are your duties there?"

"I'm with the Felony Division."

"As I said earlier, I'm investigating an incident that occurred last Wednesday night in front of the Henry Grady Inn on Drayton Street. Do you know where that is?"

"I think I've driven by it, but I've never been in it."

"Do you drive by it often?"

"Not really. It's not on my usual route to work, but I sometimes drive it. It's a one-way street going north, same as Montgomery—which I usually take to the courthouse where our office is located. Why do you ask?"

"I'll get to that in a minute. Were you driving on Drayton at anytime last Wednesday night?" When he asked this question, Kohl noted for the first time a distinct frown on Scott's face.

"No, I don't think so."

"Do you mind telling me where you were Wednesday night?" Kohl noted that the frown seemed to get more pronounced with this question.

"No, I don't mind telling you. I left the office about five-thirty and stopped by my gym for a workout. Was there perhaps an hour and a half and then went to my apartment. I believe I stopped by Subway on the way. I was home well before eight and stayed there the rest of the night."

"Did not see or call a friend, perhaps a girlfriend that night?"

"My girlfriend is in Europe, so no, I didn't see or call her. I may have made a phone call, but I don't recall any. Why the questions about my whereabouts?"

"As I said, we'll get to that. Just a few more questions." Kohl removed a photo of Scott's vehicle from the investigative file on his desk and showed it to Scott. It was the photo taken by the patrol officer early Friday morning, in Scott's parking space. "Is this your vehicle?"

Scott looked at the photo with narrowed eyes. "Yes, my Z28, my license plate."

Kohl then showed Scott the photo taken in front of the Henry Grady Inn immediately after the assault. "And this photo?"

"Yes, the same."

"Your vehicle." It wasn't so much a question as a statement.

"Yes. What does my vehicle have to do with this?" Scott asked in an agitated tone.

"Did you give anyone permission to drive your vehicle Wednesday night?"

"No. It's the only thing of any real value that I own. Unless it's an emergency, no one drives my Camaro. And so far I haven't had an emergency."

"Could anyone have stolen—or perhaps gone for a joy ride—in your vehicle Wednesday night?"

"Absolutely not. I always lock it. And always attach a locking device—The Club—to the steering wheel."

"So you are absolutely sure no one else drove your vehicle Wednesday night?"

"*Yes I'm sure*!" Scott said emphatically. "Not Wednesday night or any other night. Now, do you mind telling me what this is about? I've answered your questions—now you answer mine!"

"Yes, you've answered my questions and I appreciate it. We'll get back to you with a follow-up if necessary. I thank you for coming in, Scott."

"So that's it?" Scott said, and then stood facing Kohl, both elbows bent and both index fingers pointing like a pistol at Kohl. "You call me in and ask a bunch of questions about Wednesday night, show me a couple photos of my Camaro, and refuse to explain what this is about? That's how you operate?"

Kohl stood and faced Scott. "As I said, we'll get back to you if necessary. But I have no additional questions. Thanks for coming."

Scott squeezed his fists tightly—and walked out.

Scott left Kohl's office both mystified and angry. Just what was that about? Was it somehow connected to his being relieved from the Gordon case? He had received no explanation for that action, and

Detective Kohl would give him no explanation for questioning him. Surely they were connected somehow, but just how, he did not have a clue.

He did not return to his office. Instead he called Bill Baldwin on his cell phone. He knew Bill would not have any answer to this puzzle, but he needed someone to talk to. Bill answered the call immediately.

"Can you meet me at the Library?" asked Scott.

"When?"

"Now. I'm at the Metro Police Department headquarters, just leaving."

"What's this about?"

"I'll explain when you get there. Can you meet me there?"

Bill detected the anxiety in Scott's voice and did not question him further. "Sure," he replied.

They arrived about the same time. No one was tending the bar and Juri was nowhere in sight. A couple of law students were seated at one end of the long bar, and Scott and Bill took their seats on the opposite end, alone. In a few minutes a substitute bartender—someone Scott recognized from the serving staff of the restaurant—arrived and took their order. During the brief conversation, he said that Juri was out on some errand but was expected soon. Scott was pleased as Juri's absence would give them a few minutes for a private conversation.

"I think I'm being investigated," Scott said.

Bill frowned. "Investigated for what?"

"That's what I don't know. Just before I called you, I was questioned—well, more of an interrogation—by a Metro detective. He wouldn't give me any explanation of why he was questioning me, but apparently it was about an incident in front of the Henry Grady Inn on Drayton Street. Wanted to know if I had driven over that way last Wednesday night. He had two photos of my car and wanted me to identify it. Asked if I had given anyone permission to drive it that night. I told him nobody drives my car but me. That was about it—said he would get back to me if he had more questions, but he refused to tell me any reason for his questions."

"Who was the detective?" asked Bill.

"Guy named Kohl. I'd never met him. He was pleasant enough, but I don't like this. Those photos of my car must mean they are focusing on me. And I don't have a clue what it's about."

"I've met Kohl but don't really know him. He's been around awhile. I haven't heard of any incident involving the Henry Grady—don't check the police blotter every day like I did years ago, but I think if it was something serious I would have heard about it." Bill picked up his beer mug with both hands and held it silently in front of him. Then he turned away from Scott and cocked his head, appearing to be in serious thought. There was a long moment before he continued.

"Is there any possible reason you can think of for him having those photos of your car?"

"None."

"Could you tell where they were taken? Parked on the street? Moving?"

"I'm pretty sure they were not taken while my car was moving. Both photos showed just the rear end of my car. The license plate was clearly visible, but I saw nothing in the background to give me a clue of when or where they were taken."

A concerned frown appeared on Bill's face, and he took a long sip of beer before responding. "I'll check with my contacts over there tomorrow. Shouldn't be hard to check on an investigation when I know the date, time and place. I'll call you. But I don't think you should be worried. You'd obviously already know something about all this if they had any reason to focus on you. Lots of names find their way into an investigation when it begins. Probably just a routine interview to remove you from any further consideration."

Scott was a bit relieved hearing Bill's assessment, but he wasn't sure why. The questions from Kohl were indeed focusing on him. He was pleased Bill would check it out. That was one reason he called him. The other was he just needed someone to discuss this with, and his fellow associates at the DA's office were the last ones he wanted to tell. He wondered if he should tell Bill about being relieved from the Gordon case. Bill would find out sooner or later, but *later* would be preferred. Besides it was embarrassing, and he could give no explanation since he had received none.

Scott's eye caught some motion behind the bar. He turned and it was Juri, who saw Scott at the same time. Juri began to shake his head in a slow, sad rhythm that always followed a Braves debacle. And the previous day had been one, losing to the Diamondbacks 6-1, following a three-game winning streak.

"I thought we had something going, Scott," Juri said, as he walked over to the end of the bar where Scott and Bill were seated. "Remember back in May, we had a six-game winning streak and the Diamondbacks ended it? Now those same slimy snakes end our three-game streak. We're done. Stick a fork in us."

"Juri, they've won three of the last four. Not bad."

"Well, that's nice, but I think they're finished—and that means we should go to their *wake*." With that, Juri began to smile. "And I have tickets. The Giants—this Saturday." There was excitement in his voice.

"Remember, when Jennifer was leaving for her trip? You promised we'd drive up in your Camaro if I got some good seats behind home plate? Well, I've got 'em. Terrace Infield, Section 201, great view."

Scott began to smile, too. He hadn't been to a Braves game in quite a while. He was ready to forget the interview with Kohl.

Juri looked at Bill. "Want to come along, Bill? I can get you a ticket, maybe right in our section."

"Thanks, but I have plans. You guys are way too peripatetic."

"Too *what*?" Juri asked.

"I think he just insulted our masculinity," Scott said.

They all laughed. Bill placed some cash on the bar top and headed for the door. Scott stayed just a few minutes to discuss their upcoming trip to Turner Field and then left for his apartment. It had been an exhausting day.

Chapter Twenty

Tuesday, August 12

Carl did not lose any sleep over his failure to get the photo ID during his interview of Glenna at the Palomino. He had long ago learned that for sanity's sake, work and personal life must be kept separate. He usually slept well, even during the most exhaustive and complex investigations. But when he awoke Tuesday morning, the only thing on his mind was the investigation and the fact that he was no closer to a solution than he was Friday when he agreed to take it on. *Just what was Glenna hiding? Why wouldn't she be anxious—at least willing—to assist in the investigation of the man who attempted to pull her into his vehicle last Wednesday night?* But what bothered him most was the fact he had no clue for an answer. This investigation was going nowhere. He could not place it into any investigative matrix he had developed over the years.

Shortly after 9:00 a.m., Carl called Majewski to see if he or one of his detectives had interviewed Marino.

"Yes. Had one of our best investigators, Mike Kohl, conduct the interview. And I just listened to the tape. Nothing in it that seems to be helpful as of now. That may, of course, change. I told him not to confront Marino with any accusations—just concentrate on background info, so there was no denial or confession. Mike never told him exactly what we were investigating—just an 'incident.' After interviewing Marino, Mike went down to the Henry Grady Inn to interview the night manager. Struck out there also. He had nothing to add to his initial statement, which was simply that he heard a scream, ran outside, and saw the vehicle driving away. Now, how are things going in Atlanta—were you able to locate Monica?"

"I was, only her name isn't Monica." Carl then detailed his interview with Glenna at the Palomino Motel, emphasizing his frustration. "Something's screwy. I just can't put my finger on it. I'll be heading back to my office in Statesboro today, but I'm going to stop by the GBI Forensic Lab in Decatur on the way. I've got a couple of friends there I want to run this by—just poke around in their heads. It's a state-of-the-art lab—some pretty sophisticated equipment."

"Forensic Lab? You've got something for the lab? As far as I know, we don't have anything they could help with—a couple of photos, but we've already identified those—Marino even admits they are of his Camaro."

"Yes, I know. But they may be able to suggest something, maybe something we missed. Something we should have collected from the scene, or something we could collect now from the vehicle. I need a fresh start, John. When I agreed to get involved in this investigation, it looked like a simple two-day, maybe three-day assignment. Remember, I wanted in because Scott Marino was the suspect, and having worked with that young man, I wasn't sure I could believe the evidence unless I saw it for myself. And now this simple investigation has become too damn simple—nothing but a couple of photos and an unwilling witness. I'm looking for some fresh eyes on this *simple* investigation, and there are some smart guys and gals in that lab."

"Seems a bit unusual. What makes you think they'll do it?"

"I know two senior technicians who work there, and I'm sure they'll hear me out. I've done this before. They are pretty good sleuths. They seem to enjoy a chance to try their hand at a raw investigation."

"Well, it can't hurt. Those photos identify the vehicle, but we need . . . what's her new name? . . . eh, Glenna . . . we would have enough for a warrant if we could get her talking."

"Well, I'm not through with Glenna, but she's on hold right now, and I'm pretty much at a standstill. That's why I'm going to take a swing by the lab in Decatur—just sit down with them and pick their brains."

"Well, good luck. Keep me posted."

In the early afternoon, Carl met with his two friends, John Sokol and Patricia Toups, at the GBI Forensic Lab in Decatur. He had worked with both on previous cases, where they had testified as expert witnesses. He spent almost a half-hour explaining all that had taken place with this investigation. They appeared willing to help, in fact, anxious to help. It was a welcome break from the normal grind of the lab routine, a chance to play a different role in a criminal investigation.

When Carl completed his briefing, Sokol requested that he leave Glenna's cell phone at the lab. He also had a question regarding the camera that was used to take the photo of the vehicle at Marino's apartment complex. Carl did not have the answer but promised to get it. They shook hands, and Carl returned to his vehicle and placed a call to Majewski.

"John, the camera the patrolman used to take the photo of Marino's Camaro—that was a digital camera, right?"

"Yes, that's all we use now."

"I need you to send the digital file to the Questioned Documents Section of the GBI lab in Decatur. I'll text you a name and the email address."

"What's up, Carl? You've really stirred my curiosity."

"I'm as curious as you are, John. I'm not sure it will mean anything. But one of my lab friends, John Sokol—he's head of the Questioned Documents Section—asked for it. He didn't say why, and I didn't grill him on it. He also asked for Glenna's cell phone. I had it with me and gave it to him. I'm not counting on anything coming out of this, but I need to spend some time on another pressing investigation, and I like to think someone else is working on this one in the meantime."

"You seem to always have a pressing investigation, Carl. What is it this time?"

"Corruption. County official accused of skimming county funds—using them to set up a playhouse on Tybee Beach for his girlfriend. Came to light via the girlfriend. Seems the place wasn't as big and beautiful as he had promised. No good deed goes unpunished, you know."

"So true. Same rule could be applied to your experience in agreeing to take this case." Both laughed.

"I told my lab friend that you would get the digital file to him ASAP. I'll get back to you with anything new."

About the time Carl was leaving the GBI Forensic Lab, Scott was in his office working on a case scheduled for trial the following week. His phone rang, and it was Bill Baldwin.

"Scott, I spent some time down at the Metro Police Department this morning, checking on that incident you said happened last Wednesday. Sorry, but I hit a blank wall."

"And by blank wall you mean . . .?" Scott responded.

"I mean I came up with nothing, but I think there is something. I just couldn't find it. As you know, I have a lot of contacts there, but none of my usual sources had heard anything about an incident at the Henry Grady Inn last Wednesday or any other time recently. So I went directly to the source of your concern, Michael Kohl. As soon as I mentioned the Henry Grady Inn, his chin jerked up and his eyes narrowed. Then he said, 'That's off limits.' I said, 'What do you mean, "off limits"? Did something happen there you can't discuss?' He just replied, 'I said it's off limits,' and immediately turned and walked away. I didn't mention your name to Kohl or any of the others I talked to down there, but I'm pretty sure that whatever Kohl was investigating is being held close. Have you heard anything new?"

"Nothing. I'm as much in the dark as when I spoke to you yesterday. But thanks for trying."

"I'm not through. I have some other sources I may be able to tap later this week. I'll let you know."

"I appreciate your help, Bill, as always. Juri and I are going to leave in the early afternoon Saturday for the Braves game. I'm sure Juri can get you a good ticket—he seems to have a lot of sources. Are you sure you can't make it? We plan on driving back afterwards—not spending the night."

"Sounds like fun, but I simply can't do it. Got lots of work still to do for the Sunday edition. Enjoy the game—and I hope, for Juri's mental health, the Braves can get back on track with a win."

Chapter Twenty-One

Wednesday, August 13

Shortly after 2:00 p.m., Carl received a phone call he wasn't expecting, at least not so soon. It was from John Sokol.

"Carl, I have a report that I think you'll find quite interesting. It's about those two photos from your investigation. You told me you were having a hard time believing that young prosecutor—Marino, I believe you said his name was—would commit that assault, that you had worked with him and it simply was not believable. You sounded so positive about Marino's character."

"And I still am."

"Yet, there were the photos—same vehicle driving away from the assault as the one photographed later in the parking lot. And in an interview Monday afternoon, Marino *admitted* both photos were of his Camaro. Right?"

"Yes, that's right," Carl responded.

"I had a hunch. If with such compelling evidence, you—an experienced GBI special agent—still didn't believe he did it, then maybe there's a possibility that he didn't. I wanted to try something. That's why I requested the digital file from Savannah. I wanted to run both digital files through our Video Spectral Comparator. Are you familiar with that machine?"

"I've heard of it; not sure how it works."

"It's used primarily by forensic document examiners to detect forgeries, alterations, counterfeit items and such. It has an integrated micro spectrometer, and uses infrared, ultraviolet, and other light sources. Zoom magnification goes up to 175 times—all functions controlled by its built-in software, using a mouse and keyboard. Patricia operates it, and I can have her explain the more technical details if you are interested."

"No, I'll take your word—it's advanced technology. I just want to know what it *does* and what it *did*—if anything—in my case."

"OK, we'll skip the tech details. In brief, what we can do with it is take two documents, compare them and tell you almost anything you want to know about them. To the naked eye—even the eye of an experienced document examiner—they may look identical, but put them in that machine, and multiple differences are often discovered. That's what happened in your case."

"What do you mean?"

"When Patricia analyzed the two photos, she found multiple differences."

"Multiple differences? Like what?"

"Like you have photos of two completely different vehicles. Carl, someone obviously was trying to set up that young prosecutor."

Chapter Twenty-Two

Wednesday, August 13

Carl was momentarily stunned. *Two vehicles—someone trying to set up Marino.* It took him a while to respond.

"But John, both had the same license plate." And as soon as he said it, he wished he hadn't. Of course, they had the same license plate number—that was obvious. He quickly followed up. "I'm really a bit lost for words, John. Not sure I can ask an intelligent question, so please, give me the details."

"Well, I don't know any of the details about any of the actors or how the scene at the Henry Grady Inn was put together, but it wasn't with the vehicle that was photographed in the parking lot. The only thing that was the same was the license plate—the *only* identical thing in the two photos. My guess is that it was removed from the Camaro in the owner's parking lot and placed on the other vehicle, which was identical in color and style. To the naked eye, the same vehicle. In fact, you tell me that even the owner—Marino—said both photos were of his vehicle. But when analyzed in our lab, it was clear that the vehicles were different, only the license plate the same. That took some clever planning."

"So I've been chasing my tail for three days. Anything else you can tell me about the analysis?"

"Yes, the tires. Both photos caught part of the right rear tire. I'm sure you know that we couldn't just enlarge the photographs enough to identify the tread—it becomes distorted. But with the digital files, our machine can. We got images—not great, but good enough—to run in our TreadMate data base. You are familiar with TreadMate, aren't you?"

"If that's the computer program that can ID tire treads by manufacturer, yes. It was used in a homicide case we had in Effingham County a couple years ago. Was key evidence."

"That's it. We get a TreadMate update every three months. It has over five thousand vehicle tires in it now. Visually, with the images we produced from the digital files, we could see that the tires were different. But from the TreadMate computer search, we think we have the manufacturers of both tires. Can't be completely certain—the images weren't that good—but I'll bet you a six-pack that Marino's tire is a Michelin Precision Sport. And on the other vehicle, if you ever find it, will be a BFGoodrich tire. I don't recall the model. But all of this will be in our report."

"John, I can't tell you how much I appreciate this. But I'm sure you know. When can I get that report?"

"Oh, it's almost ready now. Everything is automated. All I need to do is slap a cover letter on it and email it to you."

As soon as he hung up with Sokol, Carl was on the phone with Frank Edwards.

"Frank, I'm calling for some more help with that Savannah assault case I'm investigating. We have a break in it, and I need to interview the girl again—ASAP."

Edwards already knew about the first interview with Glenna. Carl had briefed him Tuesday. Carl explained the lab's finding of the duplicate vehicle and how it was now obvious that Glenna was part of a scheme to set up Marino for a false arrest.

"I'm pretty sure Glenna Norris isn't smart enough to plan it or put it all together. And I can't see a motive for her. But she'll know who did. I'm scheduled to be in Statesboro for the rest of the week. If you can pick her up, I'll drop whatever I'm doing, hit I-16 and be there in three hours. You think you can bring her in?"

"No problem. One of our specialties. I'll call as soon as we have her."

It took Edwards' team less than three hours to locate Glenna and bring her in. He called Carl shortly after 5:00 p.m.

"Carl, we have your gal here at the CID Office. When do you want to interview her?"

"Tonight." Carl looked at his watch. "I'll be there about eight-thirty."

Chapter Twenty-Three

Wednesday, August 13

Carl arrived at 8:15 p.m. and was directed to a small, windowless room where he found Glenna alone, sitting in one of the three armless chairs. Besides the chairs and a small desk, the room was ringed with green metal file cabinets standing side by side against the walls. Glenna was reading from a paperback when Carl entered. She looked up at him but did not speak. Carl picked up one of the chairs and placed it a few feet directly in front of her and sat down.

"Glenna, I'm sure you remember me, Carl DeBickero of the Georgia Bureau of Investigation. We had a chat Monday night over at the Palomino Motel. I have more questions about the incident that you reported as having occurred at the Henry Grady Inn in Savannah. But first, let me tell you what I know about that incident. First, you made the report to the Savannah Metro Police. And second, we now know that your report was entirely false."

Glenna jerked her shoulders and her eyes widened at the words, "entirely false."

"I may or may not tell you how we know that, but just understand, we know it and we can prove it. And of course you know it. I understand now why you would not answer my questions the first time we talked. I could have arrested you then, but I didn't because

I wanted your cooperation. Now, I'm demanding your cooperation. Do you understand?"

Glenna did not respond but kept her eyes intensely on Carl.

"We have the evidence to put you away for a long time. But I don't want to do that because I believe you were a small player in this plot. I want to know about the major players. But if you keep up that bullshit *'I don't know'* and *'I forgot'* like you responded Monday night, we'll just put you behind bars and forget about the ones who brought it on. Do you understand the situation you are in now?"

"I think so."

"Do you know what a Miranda Warning is?"

"Uh . . . " She looked apprehensively at Carl.

"Has any police office ever read the warning to you?"

"Once. Maybe twice."

"Do you think you understand the rights it provides?"

"I think so."

"You *think* so? Well, because it's important that you *know* so, I'm going to explain them to you. And if you don't understand something I say or it's not clear, speak up. I want to make sure you understand."

Carl removed a cassette player from his briefcase and placed it on the desk.

"I'm going to turn this cassette on. We will be recorded. Move your chair over closer to the recorder, and keep your voice up."

Carl waited as Glenna moved her chair, then continued. "The time is 8:25 p.m., Wednesday, August 13, 2008. Speaking is Carl DeBickero, Special Agent with the Georgia Bureau of Investigation. I am presently in an interview room at the CID Office of the Atlanta Police Department. With me is Glenna Norris. Is that your correct name, Ms. Norris?"

"Yes."

"I am about to interview you regarding an incident you reported to the Savannah Metro Police last Wednesday night, August 6, 2008.

Glenna, prior to my turning on this cassette, were you questioned tonight about this incident?"

Glenna did not respond. She looked confused. But Carl needed a response to avoid a complaint later that he questioned her regarding the event before warning her of her Miranda rights, and thus what she was saying on the cassette was merely a repeat.

"Tonight, prior to my turning on the cassette, did you tell me anything about the incident in Savannah that you reported to the Savannah police?"

"No."

"I want you to listen to this, Glenna. *You have the right to remain silent. Anything you say can and will be used against you in a court of law. You have the right to an attorney. If you cannot afford an attorney, one will be provided for you.* Do you understand the rights I just read to you?"

"Yes."

"With these rights in mind, do you wish to speak to me?"

"Yes, OK."

"Glenna, last Wednesday you told a Savannah police officer that a man got out of a Camaro automobile and assaulted you by grabbing you by the arm as you sat on a bench next to Drayton Street. That was false, wasn't it?"

"Yes."

"I want you to tell me the truth about what happened. The whole truth."

"Um . . . I don't know where you want me to start."

"Well, let's start with how you got to Savannah."

"Ryan and Kevin, they drove me. I never was told their last names."

"Last time I interviewed you, you said you went to Savannah with one man. So it was two?"

"Yes, two."

"How did you meet them?"

"Ryan was . . . well, you know, a client—I met him a few months ago. Kevin was with him when he picked me up."

"Picked you up? You mean for the trip to Savannah? Why were you going to Savannah?"

Glenna had been sitting on the front edge of her chair. With that question, she sat back quickly in the chair. Her eyes turned toward the ceiling and closed. She remained in that position for a long while without speaking.

Carl asked again, "Glenna, why were you going to Savannah?"

Glenna lowered her head and looked directly at Carl. "Ryan, he set it up, telling me there was a thing he called a 'project' in Savannah, said he could use my help. Then he told me there was ten thousand for me if I wanted in—would take a couple days. Didn't say what it was or when. I told him I didn't want nothing to do with any drug dealings. He said it didn't involve drugs and wasn't dangerous—just that I should be ready to go when he called. He still wouldn't tell me what it was, but fuck it; I didn't care. Ten thousand dollars? Two days? Of course I wanted in. That was about three weeks ago, and when he called last Tuesday, I was ready."

"So what happened after that phone call?"

"I told Ryan I wanted the money before we left for Savannah. He agreed to pay half up front and half after we finished the job. He picked me up Wednesday and he had the cash—five thousand in big bills. I counted it out and hid it at my place. Then we left for Savannah. Ryan was driving, and Kevin was up front with him. This was the first time I ever met Kevin, but he seemed to be in charge. On the way he told me what I was to do and say when we got there. We stopped at a fast food place, and then they checked me in at this little motel or inn or whatever. I guess it was about seven o'clock. They told me to stay in my room until they got back."

Carl noticed that she seemed more comfortable responding to him than at first. "Did they say where they were going?" he asked.

"Nope. And they didn't get a room there either. I don't know where they went. I didn't see them again until sometime after ten o'clock. They came to my room and we went over again what I was to do. Then we went outside. Ryan's car was parked on the street in front of the place. They had a cell phone and took a picture of the back of the car. They checked to see if it was a good photo, then gave me the cell phone. Ryan got into the driver's seat and Kevin got in the back seat and got down, hiding. I sat down on the bench and did exactly what they had planned."

"And what was that?" asked Carl.

"I screamed as loud as I could. They waited until they saw someone running down the steps toward me, then they took off. I called 911 with the cell phone, like I was supposed to do, and told them I had been attacked."

Carl knew from the police report most of what happened after that but wanted to hear more about the two major players. "When did you see Ryan and Kevin next?"

"After the police got through questioning me, I went to my room and waited. I guess it was about an hour later, Kevin came to my room to get me, and then we walked a couple of blocks to a side street where Ryan was waiting with the car. Then we drove straight back to Atlanta."

"Did they pay you the rest of the money?"

"Yes, cash, when they dropped me off. And that was the last time I ever saw them. They told me to keep my mouth shut, and if anyone ever contacted me, I was supposed to say I was drunk and didn't remember anything about it."

"Glenna, like I said, you are facing some serious charges. But we prefer to charge the two guys behind this, not you. But if you can't help us locate them, you're left holding the bag. You understand that, don't you?"

"I do, but I don't know any more than I've told you. I'd never seen Kevin until he came with Ryan. And I don't know their last names, and even their first names might not be real."

"You said you met Ryan a few months ago and he was a 'client.' You must have his phone number somewhere—it will be on your cell phone."

"My cell phone was stolen a couple of weeks ago. I've been using a friend's house phone for my contacts. Ryan told me I could have the cell phone he took the car photo with, but the Savannah police took it."

Carl did not believe for a minute that her cell phone had been stolen, but he saw this conversation was going nowhere fast. He did have the cell phone that "Ryan" gave her, and since it was a new purchase, "Ryan" likely could be traced through the information that the cell phone number could provide. But it would take time, plus a warrant. He gave Glenna his card, with instructions to call him with any information that would help locate "Ryan" or "Kevin." He made sure she understood that if they did not locate them, she would take the fall alone.

Carl walked out of the room and placed a call to Frank to update him and thank him for locating Glenna and bringing her in.

"Did you book her?" asked Carl.

"No, just brought her in for you."

"Good. I'll release her for now. Glad you know how to find her—may have to do this again soon."

Carl drove home to Statesboro thinking of his next move. He would get a warrant to get the cell phone information from AT&T, the iPhone network carrier. Hopefully, that would lead to the ID of either Ryan or Kevin. And he had another plan—find the second vehicle. It was a black, 1984 Camaro Z28, identical to Scott's. It was unlikely that Ryan or Kevin owned one, or any close friend had one that they could borrow. Glenna said she was first approached about three weeks ago, which means that it was either recently stolen or purchased. He would have one of his assistants check Georgia law enforcement interagency files for recently stolen Camaros and the Georgia DMV for recently sold or registered Camaros. That wouldn't take long—not likely many black 1984 Z28s would be among them. But that assumed that the theft or sale occurred in Georgia. It could have occurred in any state and that would take longer. Internet auto trading sites might also turn up something—Autotrader, Cars.com, Carmax, etc.—easy to look for any make, model, and color. He would put someone to work on that also. What bothered him most was motive. *Why would anyone go to this trouble to frame Scott Marino?*

Chapter Twenty-Four

Thursday, August 14

Early the next morning, back in Statesboro, Carl placed a call to Detective Majewski in Savannah and briefed him on the second interview with Glenna. They agreed that they should brief the DA as soon as possible and that Majewski would set up the appointment. Majewski called the DA's secretary, Janna O'Meara, to set up the appointment.

"I'll check. Hold on." She was back on the phone in less than a minute.

"Mr. Magidson would like to see you this morning. Can you be here by eleven?"

Statesboro was just over an hour away, so Carl would have time to drive down. "Sure. At eleven," replied Majewski.

Carl and Majewski were called into the DA's office promptly at 11:00. Present when they arrived were the DA and Felony

Chief Joe Fasi. They shook hands and were seated. Carl knew both Magidson and Fasi, having previously worked with both of them.

Magidson turned to Majewski. "I understand you have something new on the investigation you briefed us on last week."

"We do. As you suggested, I asked the GBI to assist and Special Agent DeBickero has taken the lead in the investigation. I think it best to get the update straight from him," Majewski said, extending a hand toward Carl.

Carl spent fifteen uninterrupted minutes explaining each step in the investigation, beginning with how he located Glenna, his first interview with her, the unexpected results from the GBI Forensic Lab in Decatur, and the second interview with Glenna.

"It's quite clear now that Scott Marino was not involved in this incident and that someone or some group devised an elaborate plan to set him up for a false arrest. Other than the female, Glenna Norris, we do not know who was involved, but we have begun to follow the evidence we have, and I believe we will be able to eventually locate all involved."

Neither Magidson nor Fasi spoke when Carl was finished. The DA turned to look towards a large window and the blue, clear sky outside. Fasi turned towards the entrance, his eyes focused on a photo of one of Savannah's squares on the wall near the door. Their faces were expressionless. The room was completely quiet. Then Magidson turned to face Carl.

"Who knows about this investigation?"

"Those of us actually involved in it, of course," Carl said. "And Sokol and Toups from the Forensic Lab. And the Atlanta police detective who helped locate Glenna Norris. But I cautioned everyone to keep this confidential. It hasn't made it to any news media, I'm fairly sure."

"Good. And let's keep it that way," Magidson said. "I guess you two know how relieved I am to learn this young assistant was not involved. But we took some serious action against him that we now have to undo. We accepted the rather compelling evidence we heard in this office last week and relieved him without explanation of an important case he had been working on. Under the circumstances, I believe that was the proper action—and I would do it again with such evidence. But as it turns out we were wrong. And Joe, I believe you told me he took it very hard, especially since you couldn't tell him the reason." The DA stopped and looked at Fasi.

Fasi nodded his head in agreement.

Magidson turned again toward the large window. He stroked his chin for a long moment. "Joe, we have to make it right. We have to unring the bell. I'm not sure we can, but we have to try."

Magidson picked up his phone and dialed a number. There was a quick pickup on the other end.

"Scott, this is Josh. If you don't have a visitor with you—or a pressing trial matter—could you come to my office now?" There was a short pause, and Magidson turned to the others. "Scott is on his way here. I would like you two investigators to explain the events pertinent to the investigation from the beginning. I want him to fully understand the reasons why we took the action we did."

A few minutes later Scott entered with a pen and small note pad.

"Scott, I know you are acquainted with these two gentlemen," Magidson said, extending a hand in the direction of the two investigators. "And please be seated." Scott took a seat in an arm chair next to Fasi.

After a rather uncomfortable pause, Magidson continued, looking at Scott. "I know you have questions concerning your being relieved from the Gordon case, and I believe you are entitled to a full explanation. I was the one responsible for that action. I had received some disturbing news implicating you in a serious criminal investigation. I am pleased now to have learned that you were not involved in that incident. I've asked Carl and John to brief you on the information we received and the investigation that followed."

Scott had been sitting on the front of his chair, looking at Magidson as he spoke. As soon as he realized the full impact of what the DA was telling him, he sank back into his chair and quickly looked at DeBickero, then to Majewski and then back to Magidson, as his face tensed.

Majewski began, detailing the information he had provided Magidson and Fasi the previous Friday, displaying the photo of the Camaro taken in front of the Henry Grady Inn and the photo taken of Scott's Camaro at his apartment. Carl followed with the salient details of the investigation after he took over the lead, emphasizing the key work by the two GBI Lab employees who broke the case and his follow-up interview with Glenna who revealed how the hoax was planned and executed.

Scott remained far back in his chair, listening intently, and even though he retained the small note pad and pen in his hands, he did not take any notes. He did not look at the investigators while they spoke and kept his head slightly bowed, his eyes seemingly focused on the bottom of the DA's desk in front of him. He would frequently cross his arms for a few minutes, then unfold them and rest them on the arms of the chair. Fasi observed him closely, unsuccessfully trying to read his emotions. Whether he was pleased, angry, or resentful, he could not tell.

When Carl finished, Magidson asked if Scott had any questions. After a long pause, he shook his head slowly and said he did not.

"I know this has been a painful week for you, Scott, but I want you to know that this investigation has been held strictly on a need-to-know basis. Only Joe and I are aware of it—no one else in the office. And the investigators have been careful to ensure nothing about this has been available to the media. It should be considered as if it never happened. We want you to return to all the cases you had before this occurred. As I've said, it was me, not Joe, who removed you from the Gordon case. So, I'm sending the Gordon case back to you if you want it." The DA looked at Scott for a reply.

The reply did not come immediately. He shifted in his chair and turned his eyes to look out the window. He needed time to digest what had really happened. At first what the DA had done—and why—seemed to make perfect sense. Then it made no sense at all. They never got his side of the story before taking action to relieve him, which he now knew was just preliminary to firing him. If they could take such action so summarily, what did they really think of him and his character? Fasi knew him better than Magidson, had seen his work, had frequent, often daily contact, and had sat with him at Harrison's murder trial. He did not speak at *this* meeting; Scott wondered if he had said anything at the *previous* meeting when the DA instructed Fasi to relieve him of the Gordon case. *Did he now really want to get back into the Gordon case? Did he even want to continue in the DA's office after being so summarily treated?* In the last twelve months he had received two significant job offers from Savannah civil firms, both with much higher salaries, and he was sure he could easily find employment as a criminal defense attorney here. Or he could open his own firm. And he was sure he could find employment as a prosecutor in another jurisdiction. Taking the Gordon case and fitting back into the felony section with an overload of cases and the modest salary awarded assistant district attorneys was not his only option.

Scott remained silent, still looking toward the window. The DA waited for a reply that did not come. Eventually, the DA looked directly at Scott and said, "I know this has been a tough week, and today we've given you a lot of facts to digest. So why don't you think about it until tomorrow. Or take the weekend, and let Joe know by Monday if you want to take on the Gordon case. I believe you were lead counsel; that would again be yours if you decide you want it. Right, Joe?"

"Yes, that's right," Joe replied.

"Carl, I believe you were working that case with Scott," Magidson said. "Anything new on it during the past week?"

"Nothing new. And I'd be very pleased to see him back on the case. We work well together," Carl said, with a broad smile in Scott's direction. Scott returned a brief smile but still said nothing.

"Sounds like a good team. Scott, let Joe know when you decide." The DA stood, indicating the meeting was over.

Scott was aware that some response was required, but all he could think to say was, "Thank you, sir."

Scott walked down the long hall to his office, and by the time he was seated behind his desk he had made up his mind. He would give two weeks' notice on Monday.

Chapter Twenty-Five

Saturday, August 16

Scott had his Camaro serviced on Friday in preparation for the trip to the Braves game. Saturday promised to be a hot muggy day in Savannah, with the high reaching into the low 90s and similar weather throughout Georgia. With a twenty-four-year-old vehicle, the air conditioning—and any of the other systems—could break anytime, and a malfunctioning air conditioning system would ensure a miserable trip, or even a cancellation. Scott was extremely conscientious in maintaining the Camaro. He trusted only a few mechanics to perform any work on it, one being Gus, an elderly gent at East Bay Motors. Gus had checked everything, with special attention to the air conditioning system, and declared the Camaro ready for the trip.

Scott picked up Juri a little after 1:00 p.m. With the game scheduled to start at 7:00 p.m., they could have a leisurely drive up I-16 and then to I-75, make a couple of quick stops for gas and snacks, and arrive well before game time. Juri wanted to be there for the pre-game warmup and the national anthem—especially the anthem. He always watched the games on TV—or at least had the TV behind the bar tuned to the games—but the singing of the anthem was rarely shown, usually replaced with a beer or automobile ad. He had attended many Braves games over the years, and one of the highlights of a visit to Turner Field was to watch a celebrity stand in midfield and belt out his or her own rendition of the "Star Spangled Banner." Some great, some less so, but all delivered with great courage and ardor and always appreciated by Juri.

Scott had not planned to tell Juri of the Henry Grady Inn incident. Juri was not aware of his being relieved of the Gordon case or of anything involving the investigation. But with Scott's decision to give his two weeks' notice to the DA on Monday, Juri would soon find out. So why not? It seemed to be the perfect time and place.

They were about a half hour into their journey and traffic was light. The cruise control was set. It was a beautiful sunshiny day outside—hot, but inside the Camaro, it was comfortable. The Camaro's air conditioning system was performing just as Gus said it would. Scott began his story with Friday, the day Fasi informed him of his relief from the Gordon case. He explained that his relief came without explanation, even after imploring Fasi for one. Then he told of the examination at the Metro Police headquarters on Monday by Michael Kohl, and the two photos Kohl had of his Camaro, and again no explanation offered by Kohl of why he was being questioned.

Juri was turned toward Scott, listening carefully, but not interrupting with questions. Scott occasionally turned to make eye contact or to emphasize something he felt important. He explained being called into the DA's Office Thursday and finding Carl DeBickero and John Majewski there, along with the DA and Joe Fasi. He told Juri everything he could recall from that meeting. Juri listened intently but still asked no questions.

"I'm turning in my resignation Monday," Scott said, as he finished telling about Thursday's meeting.

Concern spread over Juri's face, and he grasped his ear as if he wasn't sure what was said. "Are you serious? You gonna quit?" Juri asked.

"I don't like the word 'quit,' but I guess that's what it is. I'm giving two weeks' notice. My contract calls for that."

"What will you do?"

"I'm not sure. I had a couple of job offers from civil law firms after the Harrison murder trial, but I'm not sure they're still open. Morrie Goldman—he's a senior partner in one of Savannah's top firms—invited me in for an interview. Essentially promised me a job. Said in two years or less I would be making double what I'm making now. I'm not sure that's what I want to do, but financially I would be better off at any civil firm than where I am now. Maybe I'll open up my own criminal defense firm."

"But you won't be leaving Savannah, will you?" Juri looked apprehensively at Scott.

"No, I don't plan on leaving Savannah, and can't, at least not until Jennifer finishes law school next May. We'll make that decision later. Next week, I'll start looking for my next job, and it will be in Savannah or close by." Scott paused just a moment, then added, "Do you want fries with your Big Mac?" Juri laughed along with Scott but then was silent for a long time before responding.

"I sure am sorry this all happened. You seemed to like your job, and you were good at it. Any chance you'll change your mind?"

"Nah. I've given it careful thought. Neither the DA nor Fasi stood up for me when those accusations were presented. They just assumed they were true. I've been there for over two years, worked with Joe at trial, and he's seen my work and observed my character. But some prostitute from Atlanta comes down for the evening, makes some false claim against me, and I get tossed without explanation. No, that's not the place I want to work."

Their conversation continued about employment possibilities; old criminal trials that Scott had prosecuted, including the Harrison trials; quirky criminal defense attorneys; and recent and unusual events at the Library Bar. Eventually the conversation got around to the Atlanta Braves and remained about the Braves for the rest of the journey.

They arrived well in advance of the first pitch and were pleased to see that Chipper Jones, who had often been sidelined with knee, back, or shoulder injuries, was in the lineup. It was a balmy 78 degrees, and the stadium was packed—over forty thousand. The Braves got off to a 8-0 lead, thanks in part to a two-run homer by Greg Norton and stellar pitching by Mark Hampton. And they remained in control, winning 11-5 and ending a five-game losing streak.

"Time to celebrate!" Juri said after the Giants hit into a double play, ending the game.

Scott was in full agreement. He had a ravishing appetite and had already selected a restaurant where he planned to order a big steak and taste some of Atlanta's craft beers: Colosimo's—"Diamond Jim's" restaurant out at Buckhead. Scott had been curious about it and its 1920s decor since his friend Grady had described it. After clearing the traffic at the stadium, it was a short drive, less than twenty minutes.

There was a twenty-minute wait for a table, and Scott took that time for a self-directed tour of the restaurant, which with its four dining rooms and its long, wide hallways, was a significant undertaking. It was as Grady described, quite garish, with an authentic Chicago "Roaring Twenties" look—marble-topped furniture, Italian tapestries, glazed chintz draperies, copper wall sconces, and slag glass lamps on each dining table producing just enough light to read the menu. The dining rooms all had Victorian gaslight chandeliers, though Scott could not tell whether they were simulated or real. Waiters wore formal attire—black trousers; long sleeve white shirts; black, button-front vests; and black bow ties. The waitresses were dressed similarly, except they wore black shorts so revealing they seemed to end where they started. The hall walls were decorated with photos of Chicago in the 1920s—speakeasies, gangsters, flappers in various costumes—at least half of which were semi-nudes—and warehouses full of barrels of bootleg whiskey, some showing federal agents with axes, hovering over barrels that were gushing moonshine onto the warehouse floor. There was a large photo of what was claimed to be one of the two hundred brothels owned and operated by the original "Diamond Jim" Colosimo. A lighting track ran above, and individual lights illuminated all the photos.

In a large vestibule near the restaurant entrance were numerous photos and biographical information of Chicago's "Diamond Jim." It showed a large man with slicked back dark hair and a wide and broad black moustache covering at least a quarter of his face. He was wearing a dark wool suit coat with a V-neck waistcoat, white shirt, and dark bow tie. Several photos showed his large hands, with enormous diamonds decorating most of his fingers. The largest photo was approximately five feet high and three feet wide. And as Grady had promised, the bio beneath it attested that "Diamond Jim" died in a hail of gunfire by someone tied to the mob. What impressed Scott most was that the bio wasn't merely printed and framed, but was *engraved* on a large heavy brass plate with quarter-inch black lettering. *A bit of an overkill even for this "Roaring Twenties" themed restaurant*, Scott thought.

Juri waited in the large, lavishly-furnished bar for the availability of their table in one of the dining rooms. He was more interested in the bar's milieu and operation than in the hallway decor. He leafed through the restaurant's ten-page wine list. He had visited Bern's Steak House in Tampa and had seen its impressive wine list of 6,500 selections. The Colosimo's list was minuscule by comparison but still impressive. The least expensive bottle was fifty dollars, with most priced around a hundred. Some, like Caymus Estate Cabernet and Opus I, were in the hundreds. A few had prices in the thousands. Juri wondered if anyone actually ordered wine for a thousand dollars a bottle at any Atlanta restaurant or if it was merely for show.

When he received notice that their table was ready, he left the bar to find Scott, who still had not completed his tour of the hallways.

They were escorted to a small table in the Capone Room, the largest dining room. Colosimo's restaurant featured beer from Chicago's Mickey Finn's Brewery. Both ordered an oatmeal stout named Pint O'Porridge, which Juri had heard of but never sampled. It was excellent. He made a mental note to see if he could find a distributor and add it to his menu at the Library Bar. This was followed by their steak orders. Both ordered one of the house specialties and the steaks were superb. They sat enjoying their beer and steaks, discussing the game they had just watched at Turner Field and the Braves' chances for making the playoffs this year or next. It was a perfect ending to a perfect day. The only downside—and a minor one— was a strolling violinist dressed in fashionable 1920s attire. There was a note attached to the menu that the violinist was there "for your dining pleasure and he is not to be tipped." He was quite talented, but he just seemed to appear too frequently and hover at their tableside, which stopped their conversation.

They had finished their meal and just finished paying the check when there was a disturbance at a table on the other side of the dining room. A lady seemed to be shouting for help, but at first they could not make out just what she was saying. Juri stood up from the table, and then clearly heard her shout, "He's choking . . . choking, help, somebody please!" Two waiters were nearby, and one appeared to be holding onto a man to steady him. The other just seemed to be glancing around the room. The lady was frantic, still shouting for help.

Within seconds, Juri was at her table. The middle-aged man was obviously in great distress. He was bent forward with both hands clutching his throat. Juri turned his face into the man's face and could see his painful expression. His eyes were opened wide with a fixed stare. He could not speak. Juri turned to the waiter who was standing behind the man, and said, "Move! And call 911."

The waiter quickly jumped backward, and Juri moved behind the man and administered a quick forceful slap between the man's shoulder blades with the heel of his right hand. Nothing was coughed up. He waited a second or two and then gave another. After five such slaps, still nothing was dislodged from his throat and he remained in serious distress. Juri could see his lips were beginning to turn blue. The lady was apparently not in a position to see the change of color, as she had quit screaming. She stood frozen nearby, with wide eyes and tight lips and her arms firmly clutching her chest.

Juri moved behind the man and locked his arms around his waist just below the rib cage. Grasping his hands together, he placed the underside of one fist in the middle of the man's abdomen, thumb-side against the abdomen, and made separate inward and upward thrusts. On the third thrust, the man jerked, and a small piece of his dinner steak was dislodged from his throat. He spit it out. Juri eased him on to a nearby chair. The man was now breathing heavily but no longer showing serious signs of distress. The lady, apparently his wife, moved to comfort him. Juri remained nearby until he was sure his assistance was no longer needed.

A small crowd had gathered to watch. Soon, paramedics were on the scene and began examining the man. One of the paramedics asked the crowd to please leave the area. As the crowd began to disperse, someone whom Scott had seen only once before, appeared.

It was James Colosimo. "Well, well, well. *Mr. Marino*," he said. "What do we owe the pleasure of this visit from the Savannah DA's office?"

Scott was not especially surprised to see Colosimo. He knew that Colosimo, as owner, could possibly be at the restaurant during the visit. But he had not seen him during his twenty-minute tour before dinner and would have missed him had the near tragedy not occurred in his dining room.

"I came for a steak dinner." Scott extended his hand toward Juri and continued. "My friend, Juri, came to save one of your customers from choking to death. Your waiters seemed to be clueless."

Colosimo looked over at Juri, who was standing near the paramedic team that was tending to the choking victim. "Yes, I saw him help the man. But, I must say I'm surprised to see *you* here after hearing of your recent incident down in Savannah."

"What recent incident?" Scott quickly replied.

"Oh, come now. We have sources for the information. Your little late-night visit last Wednesday was caught on camera. I don't want to embarrass you. I'm just curious of the status of the investigation."

Scott gave Colosimo a searing look as the words sunk in. *So this is the man responsible for the setup at the Henry Grady Inn!* He found himself breathing faster and deeper, and he could feel his anger overtaking his thoughts. He knew he must control himself. *Take it easy, Scott,* he tried to tell himself. *Stay cool, Scott.* But it was no use.

"So you're the son-of-a-bitch that set it up! You fucking slimy bastard!" Scott shouted, as he clenched his fist and stepped toward Colosimo. And just as suddenly, a man appeared at Colosimo's side, and Colosimo stepped behind him. Then another man appeared at his side, and within seconds half the wait staff of the restaurant had appeared and formed a wall around Colosimo.

Juri had heard and observed the entire confrontation. He rushed over and grabbed Scott by the arm. "Don't do it, Scott. We're way outnumbered. This is their turf. Let's get out of here."

Scott did not move and neither did the opposition. They all stood silently, immobile, glaring. Then with both hands on Scott's shoulders, Juri firmly pushed him toward the exit. Scott was not resisting but neither was he leaving willingly. Colosimo and his assistants did not follow, and soon Scott and Juri were out of the restaurant. They got into the Camaro and headed south on Peachtree, with Scott behind the wheel.

"Juri, sorry we had to leave. You didn't even get a 'thank you' for saving that guy's life. If we had stayed maybe you would have gotten a meal voucher." Scott looked over at Juri with a grin. "But you were awesome. He was turning blue, and he would surely have died right there had you not taken charge. Where did you learn that?"

"Signed up for a first aid class that taught it. Everyone in the restaurant business should know how to treat a choking victim. Should be a requirement for a permit."

"Well you obviously learned the procedure well. He owes you his life."

"Yeah, but I didn't follow all the recommended steps. As I recall them now, I believe I was to ask the guy if he was choking, tell him I can help, and then get his damn permission to assist before slapping him on the back. I think that's to keep from getting sued if the procedure fails. I recall wondering during the instruction if that really could be followed—now I know. I heard the lady shouting, 'He's choking. Help!' And the guy was grabbing his throat and turning blue. So, I'm supposed to say, 'Sir, you appear to be in serious distress, are you perhaps choking, maybe got something stuck down in your throat?' And he says, 'Now that you mention it, sure appears that way.' And then I say, 'Well, I'm trained in a procedure that is frequently used to assist choking victims. Would you like me to assist you?' And he says, 'I think that would be a marvelous idea. Where do I sign?'"

Scott laughed, "I don't think that would have worked tonight. You did good, Juri. No question that if you hadn't taken charge with some quick action, that would be the last steak that guy would ever see."

"That man you called a 'slimy bastard'—that was the restaurant owner, Colosimo? Max Gordon's attorney?"

"That's him," Scott replied.

"You should have called him a '*cheap* slimy bastard'—like you said, no meal voucher, not even a drink offer at the bar. Do you suppose we did something that pissed them off?"

Scott laughed but did not respond. They drove south on I-75 in silence. Juri knew Scott was now in deep thought and decided it best not to interrupt him. It was now a little after midnight and traffic on the Interstate was light. Scott was maintaining a steady speed of about 65 mph, and Juri found himself dozing off occasionally. At Macon—about an hour south of Atlanta—they took I-16, which would take them to Savannah. They had gone only a few miles on this new Interstate when Scott startled Juri by smacking the center of the steering wheel hard with an open palm, and exclaiming, "I've decided!"

Juri sat up in his seat and turned toward Scott. He had just dozed off, and it took him a long moment to respond. "Decided what, Scott?"

"I'm going back to the DA's office and take over the Max Gordon trial. I want to watch that *cheap* slimy bastard and his slimy client when the jury brings in the verdict. I want to be right there, I don't want to just read about it."

"Good decision. That's where you belong."

"Apparently the DA and my boss, Joe Fasi, at least for a while, didn't believe so."

"I've been thinking about that, Scott. With what they knew then, I think they took the right action. They had a responsibility to do it. They had a photo of your car with your license plate clearly showing. No one else drives it. You said so yourself. And the young lady—the so-called victim—she ID'd you from your driver's license photo. What else could they think? They obviously respected you or they would have arrested you on the spot. And one other thing I've been thinking about. You told me you heard Max Gordon tell his attorney as they were leaving the courtroom, to 'get that arrogant son-of-a-bitch off the case.' Did you ever tell Fasi or the DA about that?"

"No."

"Well, you should have; it may have made a difference. When they got that initial investigative report, they may have said, 'Hey, wasn't Max Gordon out to get Scott from the get-go? This thing at the Henry Grady doesn't sound like the Scott we know. Maybe this is a setup.' But they didn't have that possibility to consider. You're being way too unforgiving. They did what they had to do. That's my take on it."

Juri looked at Scott as he spoke, and Scott occasionally turned to make eye contact, which was difficult in the dim light. But he did not respond, and Juri did not speak further.

They were almost to Savannah when Scott finally spoke. "Juri, you are right. They did what they had to do. I should be grateful—and I am."

Chapter Twenty-Six

Monday, August 18

Scott was in his office by 7:30 a.m. Monday. He wasn't sure of the protocol for what he had to do that day, but he knew he had to do it. The task—informing Joe Fasi of his decision regarding the Gordon case—was heavy on his mind. He had plenty of work to do on his other cases and decided there was no rush. That task could wait until the afternoon, and he would keep it as low-key as possible. He would not explain any of his reasons and did not expect any further explanation from his boss. He would just try to take up where he left off.

The issue was resolved painlessly and more quickly than he expected. Fasi entered his office with a large file.

"Here's the Gordon case, Scott. I hope you are ready to take it again. You are still lead counsel, and I'm ready to assist as second chair—just let me know how I can help."

Scott took the file from Fasi and said, "Thanks. I hope you'll do the jury selection. That's still my weakest part, and you are good at it."

"Sure, I'll take it. I actually enjoy jury selection. I think you will too, eventually."

"Well, I'm getting plenty of practice in my other cases, just not there yet."

"Keep me posted on this case. Josh has a special interest in it. I'm sure he'll be wanting me to update him soon." Fasi began to walk toward the door, then turned. "And let me know when you hear from his attorney—'Diamond Jim' I believe you call him?"

"No, I don't call him 'Diamond Jim.' He would *prefer* that I call him 'Diamond Jim,' but the last time I saw him, which was Saturday night, I called him a 'slimy bastard.' I think you should hear how that came about. Why don't you have a seat, and I'll tell you about it."

Fasi gave Scott a puzzled look and walked over to a chair beside Scott's desk and sat. Scott began by telling him briefly of the trip to Turner Field for the ball game. Then he gave a detailed report of their visit to Colosimo's, the choking incident, and the appearance of "Diamond Jim" and his question about the "little late night visit that was caught on camera."

"I was ready to give him a Tennessee knuckle sandwich, but he ducked behind one of his goons. And then, we were quickly outnumbered by about eight to two. Juri ushered me out and we headed back to Savannah. Guess I was lucky—I might be calling from Atlanta about now, asking for you to bail me out of the Fulton County Jail."

Fasi had listened intently as Scott relayed the story, shaking his head slowly as Scott ended.

"No way Colosimo could have any information on the incident unless he or someone working for him organized it. The investigation was strictly confidential," Fasi said.

"Bill Baldwin can vouch for that," Scott said. "I asked him to find out why I was interviewed regarding some incident at the Henry Grady Inn. He spent a couple days asking around and came up empty—and he has good connections with a number of Savannah detectives."

"So it was obviously a set up, and Colosimo was somehow involved. We have to get this information to Carl DeBickero—he's now in charge of the investigation," Fasi replied.

"I'll brief him today. I'll be checking in with him this afternoon to discuss preparation for the trial."

"Good. And I'll brief Josh," Fasi said as he got up to leave. "He considers this one of the most important cases we have right now, and he'll be expecting weekly briefings. You are still lead counsel, but I'm involved in this trial, too, so let's plan to meet and discuss it early next week—I'll check my calendar and call you."

Fasi walked out of the door and Scott got back to his other cases. He would start work again on the Gordon case after making contact with Carl in the afternoon. He was pleased that he was still an assistant DA and once again had the lead in the Gordon case. He was even more pleased that Jennifer would be returning with her parents from their European trip this week, and he would be joining them at Hilton Head on Saturday for a celebration of their return.

Scott called Carl in midafternoon. Carl was at the GBI office in Statesboro and was pleased to hear that Scott was back on the Gordon case. Nothing had really changed in the interim, and they did not expect any big changes. There were a number of administrative matters still to attend to—preparation and service of subpoenas for example—but no new leads to chase down. And they weren't waiting for forensic reports. This was not a case where forensics would play a role—nothing to connect Gordon to the crimes except the other witnesses who were also caught up in them. Scott thought about how this trial would differ from the trials seen on TV. There would be no forensic evidence to present, no white coats to testify. He would have to convince the jury of Gordon's guilt with witnesses who the jury would know were testifying with pretrial agreements to save their own hides. But Carl had produced a solid investigation, and despite the baggage dragging behind his three main witnesses, he was still confident he could and would get a conviction.

Soon into the conversation, Scott gave Carl a report of his Saturday night visit to Colosimo's. When he was finished, Carl said, "Sounds like you were ready to rumble. I'm glad you held your cool."

"I *didn't* hold my cool. But Juri ushered me out before I did something foolish."

"That's what friends are for. At least we now have a good lead on who originated that setup," Carl said. "We haven't made much progress, but I must confess we've slowed the investigation since it became clear you weren't involved. That was my main concern—and your DA's main concern and the reason it got my top priority for a week. But after I got that report from the GBI Lab that cleared you, I moved my major effort to some other pressing investigations. But for sure, we're going to continue working it. We expect to have the results from our phone records subpoena soon."

"I don't recall if I ever told you," said Scott, "but Colosimo has two associates in his small office—both disbarred attorneys. I suspect if you could get some photos, there's a good chance the girl—I can't recall her name—could ID them."

"Glenna. Sure, we'll do that. I can pull them up from DMV records. I think I have her convinced she needs to cooperate, or she'll be taking the fall alone and eating jail rations for a year or so. And I'll have Majewski show them around to the employees at the Henry Grady Inn. Maybe get an ID there, too."

"Yeah, would be a better ID than one coming from Glenna. I seem to recall she ID'd me a couple of weeks ago." Scott paused a moment as he reflected on how he was so quickly thrust into the investigation by that false ID.

"I'll be contacting Patel's attorney, Luke Schaub, in a few days," Scott continued. "I want to make sure Patel is stable. Last time I spoke to Luke, he said Patel was almost a basket case."

A few minutes later they hung up, with Carl saying he would be in Savannah the next week on a different investigation and would give him a call.

Chapter Twenty-Seven

Thursday, August 28

Scott received a phone call early Thursday morning from Luke Schaub. "My client approved the pretrial. I'll be over your way in about twenty minutes to discuss a case I have with Daniel Mackay and can bring the pretrial by. Is this a good time?"

"Sure, come on over. I'll be here all morning."

Scott was anxious to see that it was signed by the defendant, Vijay Patel. The latest offer was for a maximum of twelve months confinement for the plea of guilty to both charges—perjury and conspiracy to commit perjury—and for testifying against Gordon. Scott had originally offered a pretrial for three years confinement, but that had been rejected. And when it became clear that twelve months was all he could expect, he relented and made the new offer. He thought the crimes deserved much more, but knew that this lower sentence was crucial to get Patel to cooperate. Limiting it to twelve months meant he could serve the sentence in the Chatham County jail, near his family—assuming he didn't completely fall apart and have to be committed to Central State Hospital in Milledgeville. Scott had not set a deadline for accepting the plea, but to encourage acceptance, it contained a clause that the offer could be withdrawn by the prosecutor anytime before it was accepted.

He had made a similar offer to Josh Johnson's attorney, Doug Noah, a few weeks back, but so far he had not heard from him. Neither Patel nor Johnson had any prior convictions or arrests. Nevertheless, Scott thought the pretrial was much too generous for the offense—perjury in a robbery case—especially since it led to freeing a man who soon robbed again and in the act killed a teenage girl. But he had to have this testimony.

Luke arrived shortly with the pretrial. Scott looked it over and was pleased to see it was approved, signed, and witnessed.

"How's your client holding up?" asked Scott.

"Hanging in there. Scared. Despondent. Pretty torn up. Has made it hard for me to discuss the pretrial and explain why it's good for him. If the only charge was perjury, I'd advise him to refuse it—take it to trial. With the two-witness rule, I don't think you could prove it. But the conspiracy is another matter. I can't see any way around it, with the photos and testimony of Wilborn. Plus, he led the GBI agent straight to where he had hidden the cash payment, and he admitted what the payment was for. So how could he beat it? But he *could* beat the perjury charge, no question. I know you think the pretrial is too lenient, and you wouldn't have offered it except you want Gordon more than the others. Just know this, Scott. Except for this one bad act, he's an exemplary citizen. Even good citizens sometimes have a limit and his was $250,000 cash. I can assure you, he is deeply remorseful."

"As he should be. Does he understand he's partially responsible for the death of a beautiful and talented teenager—on her way to college with a scholarship and hopefully into medical school?"

"I don't think so, and I'm not about to remind him. He could easily come unglued. Neither of us wants that."

"You are so right. I need his testimony, so prop him up every way he needs it. I'm not sure how a jury will respond to his testimony, knowing he got such a favorable pretrial. I'm a bit uncomfortable waiting to have him actually enter his plea until after the Gordon trial, though I doubt it makes any difference to the jury. Colosimo will make sure they know he's testifying with a plea agreement to save his ass from a much more severe sentence."

"Yes," replied Luke. "And waiting until later to enter his plea may keep him from unraveling before he has to testify."

"Does he understand the judge also has to accept the plea agreement?"

"I explained that. He said he understood. But do you think there's a chance that the judge won't accept it?"

"Of course, there's always a chance, but Judge McCabe is a former prosecutor. He'll surely understand the necessity of a pretrial like this, even if it appears too generous. I don't think there's much of a chance that he won't accept it. And if he doesn't, we'll have to drop the perjury case. That will leave the conspiracy case, and as you say, there's no way around that one. Agree?"

"Well, that's the way I see it now," said Luke.

"His co-defendant, Johnson, is still confined. Hasn't been able to make his $25,000 bail and hasn't accepted the pretrial yet. And if he does, it requires that he enter his plea *before* the start of Gordon's trial. So the jury will get the testimony from one perjurer awaiting conviction and another already convicted. Can't build a stronger case than that, can I?" They both laughed.

"Do you plan to be in the courtroom when your client testifies against Gordon?" asked Scott.

"Of course."

"Good. Should give him encouragement," Scott said. "Colosimo will rake him over. We need to get him ready. When can we three meet for trial preparation?"

"I'll check and give you a call."

Chapter Twenty-Eight

Wednesday, September 10

Scott returned to his office from a midmorning court hearing to the sound of his desk phone ringing. He laid his briefcase down and answered. It was Doug Noah, the attorney from the public defender's office who was representing Johnson. Johnson had been unable to make bail and was still confined in the Chatham County Jail to await trial.

"I'm calling about that pretrial offer. I think we can do it, if we can get Johnson's bail reduced a bit."

"How much?"

"He can make bail at $10,000."

"That's a $15,000 reduction. I'd say that's more than 'a bit.' And if he has $10,000, how does he rate a public defender? For that kind of money, he could hire Jeff Brown or David Paul—or any of Savannah's finest."

"Yeah, hire 'em for maybe a week. But anyway, it's not his money—he doesn't have any control over it. It's being put up by a friend from one of the casinos in Black Hawk, Colorado. That's where he says he lost all his money."

There was no question in Scott's mind that Johnson still had the $250,000. Somewhere. He had admitted to Carl DeBickero that he received it—and there were photos taken by Wilborn of the delivery. Scott could not believe someone who received that much in illegal funds would be out flaunting it at some casino. But the location of that money was not Scott's major interest. What he wanted was Johnson's testimony.

"So specifically, what are you asking?"

"That you agree to ask the judge to reduce his bail to $10,000. In return, Johnson will agree to plead to conspiracy to commit perjury and testify fully and truthfully against Max Gordon. Maximum sentence of one year confinement."

Scott considered it for a moment. The bail money was not his major concern; it was illusionary. The state didn't get to keep it. It was returned after the trial and sentencing were concluded, so to Scott, reducing the bail wasn't a problem. He wasn't sure of getting a conviction for perjury because the two-witness rule would come into play. But he had no question he could get a conviction on the conspiracy charge, where the rule did not apply. It really made no difference; conviction for either crime would be sufficient to support the sentence proposed. But he was going to insist that he plead guilty as charged, just as he had demanded of Patel.

"Here's the deal I can make. Nothing less," said Scott. "He pleads guilty to both charges, perjury and conspiracy to commit perjury. He agrees to testify truthfully at Max Gordon's trial. I'll agree to bail at $10,000, with ankle monitor, and travel limited to Chatham County while awaiting trial. Sentencing comes after he testifies in Gordon's trial, but he must plead *before* trial. Maximum sentence of one year confinement."

There was a long pause on the other end before Scott heard the response. "Write it up. I think he'll take it. He realizes with those photos, you have him slam-dunk for conspiracy, and that will get him up to five years."

Chapter Twenty-Nine

Monday, October 5

Vijay Patel was rearranging the beer and soft drinks in Fast Eddie's, his small convenience store on Waters Avenue in Savannah. It was 10:30 p.m., and business was unusually slow even for a Monday, which was always the slowest. As he did on many nights when there were few customers, he let his cashier off early. The trial in which he would have to testify was fast approaching and constantly on his mind. And his guilty plea and sentence would soon follow. The pressure was causing constant anxiety and many sleepless nights. His family was supportive, but he was heartsick for having caused them such embarrassment. And soon he would be a convicted felon and sentenced to the county jail for a year, and the pain he had caused his family would continue. He was weary, depressed, and he could see no end to this misery that he had brought upon himself and his family.

Two casually dressed men entered the store and walked to the beer cooler where Patel was working. One appeared to be about thirty-five years old, the other a little older, perhaps in his early forties. The younger man opened one of the glass doors of the twenty-foot-long refrigeration unit and looked in. He removed a Heineken six-pack and held it up for the older man to see. The older man nodded as if he was in agreement with the choice. Patel observed this from about ten feet.

"I can help you with that," Patel said. "I'll be over at the cash register." Then Patel walked quickly over to the service counter to wait on his two customers.

When they reached the counter, the older man threw a twenty on the counter, and Patel rang up the order and made change. Then the man carefully made eye contact with Patel, and said, "Are you perhaps the owner of this store?"

"Yes, I am," Patel responded.

"Vijay Patel?"

"Yes."

"I understand you are in a bit of legal trouble. I think we can help. Would you like to know *how* we can help?"

Patel was puzzled by the question and apprehensive at what was happening—two men entering his store and questioning him about his legal problems. "I have an attorney," he responded.

"Yes, I understand that. I believe his name is Luke Schaub. Is that correct?"

Patel was surprised and wary of the question. "Yes, and he has instructed me not to discuss my case with anyone. And I don't intend to."

"Oh, we don't want to discuss your case. Your attorney was absolutely correct in advising you not to discuss the case. But I'm sure he hasn't asked you to close your ears and your mind to information that may help. That's all we're here for. This information is free if you want to listen. We'll not ask you any questions. That's a promise. But I would think you would want to have this information—there *is* a way out of your legal problem. If you want to hear it, we will provide the information you need. If you don't want to hear it, we'll walk out the store right now. Your choice."

There was no "way out," Patel was sure, yet here was a man promising just that, if he wanted to hear it. He would not have to discuss the case or answer any questions. He was wise enough to understand the importance of Schaub's instructions and he would follow them. But what harm could come from just listening to what this man had to say? Like a drowning man clutching for any floating debris, he would listen.

"Ok, I'll hear you out. But no questions, none."

"Of course not, that was our promise. You are charged with perjury, a serious crime. And because it is such a serious crime, the law in Georgia requires not only that the prosecutor prove the charge beyond a reasonable doubt, but prove it by more than one witness. This is called the two-witness rule. That's very important to your case, Mr. Patel. For example, if you were charged with murder, the testimony of one witness—a *single* witness—would be sufficient to prove your guilt. But for perjury, two witnesses are required. I promised you I would not ask any questions, but think about it. Ask yourself, where are the two witnesses? Mr. Patel, you are simply offering yourself on a platter to the prosecutors. They can't prove you lied, but you are going to take the stand and tell the jury you lied. And you are going to do that because you think you are getting a good deal. Yes, a good deal."

The older man, who was speaking, turned to the younger man and asked, "Anderson, what is the maximum sentence for someone convicted of perjury?"

"Ten years imprisonment, minimum of one, plus a fine."

"So you are indeed getting a good deal, but a good deal only if it could be proved. And you now know it can't be proved."

Patel listened carefully. *Could there be any truth to this? Could there indeed be a way out of his problem?* He wanted to believe them. However, he kept cautioning himself not to be taken in by these two men whom he had never met.

"Of course you are wondering now why we, complete strangers are telling you this. Well, Mr. Patel, there are some of us in the community who stand for justice. And you are also wondering why your attorney has never explained this to you. We can't answer that. Perhaps he is unaware of this requirement for proof of perjury. And then again, maybe he is aware, but for some reason unknown to you, failed or refused to discuss it with you. Perhaps he is working with the prosecutor. Money moves around quickly in the criminal justice system—you experienced that yourself with that suitcase of $250,000. Or maybe it's not the money at all, but a favor your defense counsel needed from the prosecutor on behalf of another client, perhaps a wealthier client. The criminal justice system holds many secrets. Crimes have a way of reaching out and corrupting others—those who commit them, those who investigate them, those who prosecute them, and yes, even those who defend them."

A customer came through the front door as they were talking, and walked up to the counter. He asked for a pack of cigarettes, which Patel quickly produced. The customer paid and quickly left. And just as quickly, Patel took the same position across the counter to listen again to these two strangers. He had serious doubts that anything they were saying or suggesting had any truth, but he would listen.

"So, Mr. Patel, we have a solution for your problem and it is a simple, three-part plan. First, and most important, do not become a sacrificial lamb. Even though you have accepted a pretrial agreement, you are not required to testify at that trial and incriminate yourself. You have an absolute right against self-incrimination. I'm sure you know that. They cannot prove your perjury. You do not need to take our word for that, and this is the second part. I'm sure you have Internet access. Look up the 'two-witness rule.' Read it for yourself."

Patel continued to listen intently, but he remained silent. His eyes tightened in a frightened look, but in fact he was pleased with what he was hearing.

"The third part is up to you. And that is whether you should discuss this with your attorney. If you think you must, then do it, but remember, you got into this fix by listening to your attorney. Ask yourself if you can really trust him. Was he leading you to slaughter and if so, why? Will you get a truthful answer? Think carefully and weigh all the facts that you know are true. Consider what you find on the Internet, and compare it with what I've told you. Compare it with what you heard from your attorney. Then make your decision."

The man turned to his partner, and said, "I think we should be going now. Do you have anything to add?"

"No, I think you covered it all very thoroughly."

The younger man picked up the Heineken six-pack from the counter, and they both walked slowly out the door.

Patel stood at the counter thinking carefully about what he had just heard. Maybe there was a way out, but he had to think very carefully about what he should do. First, he needed to get on the Internet. He had access through his desktop computer in his small office behind the counter. He locked up, turned off the lights and went to his office to make the Internet search.

He entered "two-witness rule." Immediately, quite a few hyperlinks appeared. Several were to biblical passages and one to the United States Constitution, which required two witnesses for conviction of treason. Then he found this definition under a headline, "Two-Witness Rule Law and Legal Definition."

> **"Two-witness rule refers to the rule in many states that applies to a charge of perjury. Under this rule, two witnesses are required to establish that the alleged perjurer gave false testimony."**

That got his immediate attention. His pulse was now beating faster. Maybe, just maybe, those two strangers were right. Maybe there was a way out. He read it again and noticed the words, "in many states." Was Georgia one of those states? He thought of calling his attorney, but it was approaching midnight. And he recalled the advice of the strangers. *Could he really trust his attorney? Why was this critical information withheld from him? Was his attorney really working for him—or for the prosecutor? Was it in his best interest to even tell his attorney of this late night visit by two strangers? Would his attorney perhaps be angry at him?*

Even though he did not discuss the case, the strangers discussed the case. He was conflicted, but the decision of whether to tell his attorney could wait. He needed more time to think this through. His pressing need now was to find out if Georgia was one of those states, and he knew where he could go and confidentially find his answer: the reference librarians at the Savannah Bull Street Library. His oldest daughter had used them many times while in high school and had always spoken highly of them. They would help, and he would be there when the library opened at 9:00 the following morning. The trial was still six weeks away. He had plenty of time to decide what, if anything, to tell his attorney.

Chapter Thirty

Wednesday, November 12

The last several weeks had passed quickly for Scott. He had at least one trial almost every week, plus preparation for the Gordon case which would begin the next week. In addition, he and Jennifer were beginning to discuss marriage after her graduation in the spring. He had already selected a ring. He wondered if he was supposed to discuss their plans with her father—ask for his permission. *Did young men still do that?* Both parents were expecting them to marry, so he saw no need to ask for permission. He knew that many couples just sort of drifted into their marriage decision, but he planned to actually "propose"—maybe not actually get down on a knee, but he would present the ring and ask Jennifer to marry him—probably during the Christmas holidays. He had not yet picked the date or the place. It would not be in his personality to make a public show of it—no full-page ad in the local paper, and he wouldn't hire a skywriter to paste it over Savannah for everyone to see. This would be private and special—just the two of them—something to remember forever. Their first date was at the Library Bar and Grill, immediately after one of Jennifer's freshman orientation sessions at Savannah Law. He knew a first date site was a popular place to propose, and as much as he loved the Library, it didn't seem to be the special place that he was seeking. He would have to give it more thought.

This was a day he and Joe Fasi were to meet to make final preparation for the Gordon trial, which was to begin the next Monday. Scott felt good about his witnesses and his chances for a conviction. Like the trials that Gordon had defended involving John Harrison, this trial with Gordon as the accused had substantial media interest. Judge McCabe had approved a "Memorandum of Agreement," signed by all the media organizations that would be covering the trial. That included at least one TV station in Savannah, Atlanta, and Chicago, and they would be sharing a single camera. One still photographer would be allowed, and all photos would be pooled.

Scott arrived in Fasi's office with all the files. The office had a pleasant scent of freshly brewed coffee. Fasi thrived on coffee and had his own single-serve machine in one corner of his office. Scott, like all the other assistants, got his coffee from the community machine maintained by the secretaries and located in a small storage room. Fasi was the only one in the entire office with his own machine. He had several gourmet single-serve brands for his guests, but Folgers Columbian was always in his own cup.

Fasi motioned Scott to take a seat, then said, "How about joining me in a fresh cup of coffee before we start? What would you like?"

"Anything Starbucks."

"French Roast?"

"Perfect," Scott said.

In a couple of minutes both had a cup of coffee in their hands and were ready to get down to the day's business.

"Anything new from Carl?" asked Fasi.

"Nothing new on the case, but he called me yesterday with news on the investigation of my alleged visit to the Henry Grady Inn. Remember that?"

"Unfortunately, yes. What's new?"

"Quite a bit. Carl got a good ID from the woman, Glenna. He had photos of the two disbarred lawyers working in Colosimo's office—Thomas Reid and Anderson McDowell. She's positive they are the ones who drove her to Savannah for the setup. The cell phone purchase records also led to them. And they've already located the second car. It was purchased in Birmingham after an ad in AutoTrader. It's now registered in Reid's name, and he's still driving it. Previous owner says they paid his asking price of forty-two hundred, and they didn't bother to haggle once they saw it."

"Have they tied in Colosimo?"

"They don't have a clean case against Colosimo, at least not yet, but I expect that will be coming too. Those two reprobates won't take the fall alone. I expect them to quickly implicate Colosimo."

"So they've made an arrest of the two guys from his office?"

"No, not yet," Scott said. "I asked Carl to delay any arrest until after the trial. I don't want anything to stop the trial from getting underway. I want Colosimo in the courtroom Monday, sitting cozy next to Gordon at the defense table. Even though they weren't planning to arrest Colosimo, I expect arresting his two major assistants would have a big spillover effect. He would probably ask the judge for a delay, and he just might get it."

"I don't believe Judge McCabe would grant a delay, but it's possible. Probably a good call," Fasi said.

"I'll get more details from Carl tomorrow. He'll be stopping by my office to go over his testimony once more. He'll be my first witness. I told him he should be at the courthouse Tuesday morning. I'm skeptical that we can get a jury in one day, but I want him available just in case."

"Good, because I really believe we can get a jury Monday. McCabe will take charge and run through his stock questions rapidly, but he's pretty thorough. Unless it's a capital case, he brings the entire panel into the courtroom and questions them all together. He cuts attorneys off quickly if they try to ask a question he's already covered.

There's been *some* pretrial publicity about the case here in Savannah but certainly not like the previous Harrison trials. Gordon's home town, Chicago, has probably seen more publicity than Savannah. The legal community here is interested because a big time lawyer is on trial, but I don't think the average citizen knows or cares. I think most will say, 'Max who?' Yeah, I think we'll get a jury without any problems. What's the latest on the other witnesses?"

"They're all out on bail and so far have complied with their bail conditions. Richard Evans is keeping tabs on that. All have been served, and their attorneys tell me they haven't wavered from their initial statements. I don't see any problem there. Even Patel, who was almost a basket case, has settled down. Goes to work at his store every day. Johnson is staying in Savannah with an old army buddy. He's wearing an ankle monitor and has kept within the confines of Chatham County, as required by his bail. The judge had no problem accepting his plea and the pretrial agreement. I was a bit concerned about the pretrial, but the judge did not question it. Clarence Wilborn was allowed to go back to his home town in Macon to await trial. He's already pled—sentencing will be a few weeks after the Gordon trial. He's also wearing an ankle bracelet. Authorities in Macon are monitoring him."

"Are you still comfortable making the opening and the closing?" asked Fasi. "You said you wanted to do both, but I'm available to take one—your decision there, Scott."

"No, you'd probably screw it up." They both laughed. "And I'd screw up the jury selection. So you just pick me a good jury, and I'll be very pleased to do the rest."

They discussed the case for another hour or so, looking carefully once again at the thick investigative file prepared by Carl DeBickero and John Majewski, as well as the numerous case notes that Scott had prepared over the last few months. Fasi knew this was Scott's first trial before Judge McCabe. Fasi had tried quite a number of cases before the judge, so he was careful to explain the judge's trial philosophy and personal characteristics. Fasi explained that McCabe seemed to go out of his way to avoid any appearance of having a prosecutorial bias.

"If it's a minor issue involving evidence, and one that in his discretion could go to either side, he's likely to rule quickly, and for the defense," Fasi said. "But if it's an evidentiary issue that could devastate the prosecution case, he'll take it slow, often requiring additional research and oral argument. In the cases I've had before him, he's never shown a prosecutorial bias or prejudice."

"We could use a little prosecutorial bias on at least one issue," Scott responded.

"And that would be . . . ?"

"The corroborating circumstances for the 'two-witness rule,'" Scott said with a grin.

"Well, don't look for it," Fasi said. "He'll call 'em like he sees 'em. He's been on the bench for at least fifteen years and is seldom reversed. In fact, I've never heard of him being reversed for an error in admitting or excluding evidence."

After a second cup of coffee, the conference ended. Scott returned to his office to complete preparation on his opening statement. He was looking forward to Monday, fully confident in his case.

Chapter Thirty-One

Monday, November 17

Scott spent the weekend with Jennifer and her family in Hilton Head. It rained heavily all day Saturday, preventing their usual visit to the beach, but it did not dampen the pleasure he always found in a Hilton Head visit. They braved the rain to go to one of their favorite night spots, The Jazz Corner. And as usual, they were careful to stay out late enough to ensure that Jennifer's mom and dad had retired, giving them a couple hours of perfect time alone to end the day.

The rain departed and the sun came out Sunday. The day was bright and clear as Jennifer's father prepared the grill for the traditional Sunday afternoon cookout. This one would include a whole red snapper and fresh Capers Island oysters on the half-shell. He was amazing to watch as he presided over the grill. To Scott, it was like a magic show, and it always ended in taste perfection. But try to compliment him and the reply would always be modest, something like "Oh, it's nothing special." Scott admired the man in so many ways. Growing up in Tennessee without a father, he was now fully realizing what he had missed.

Scott and Jennifer left Hilton Head earlier than usual. Jennifer had class work waiting, and Scott needed to get home to put the final touch on his preparation for the trial, which would start Monday morning.

And now Monday had arrived, and he was sitting in Courtroom K, quite a bit early, waiting for the trial to begin. Fasi had not arrived and the defense table was vacant. He looked around the courtroom. There were no spectators, and the only others in the courtroom were a single bailiff and a two-man crew setting up a TV camera. The camera would not be on during jury selection, but the crew was there to be ready when the opening statements began.

Scott began to reminisce about the weekend he had just spent with Jennifer at Hilton Head. He mused at what a lucky young man he was. His mother had never met Jennifer, but in Scott's phone calls she had heard all about her. Jennifer would be going to Tennessee with Scott to visit his mother over the Christmas holidays. He hadn't told Jennifer of the false assault he had been accused of while she vacationed in France or the investigation that followed. He would someday, but not until this trial was over—and maybe a long time afterwards.

Scott did not see the man as he entered the courtroom and walked into the gallery, directly to the rear of where Scott was seated. But the sharp sound he made when he plopped his heavy briefcase on the pew-style wooden bench woke Scott from his reverie. He swiveled in his chair and looked. *The face was familiar, but where had he seen it?* Then he recalled. He had never actually seen the face, only a photo—a photo of a "staff member" on Colosimo's website.

He quickly suppressed an initial impulse to cause some major damage to the rogue's face—perhaps move his nose a few inches to the right. But that would not be a good start for the day. He immediately had second thoughts about the request he had made to Carl—to wait to arrest the two men who had traveled to Savannah with Glenna to frame him. *Just what could this disbarred thug have in mind, coming to this trial? Obviously more evil, more corruption. But what?* Scott did not expect to be assassinated in the Chatham County

Courthouse, but for a moment it did cross his mind, and just to be on the safe side, he decided not to give the man a clear shot to his back. He continued to face the man, who was now seated with his arms folded across his chest and staring in Scott's general direction without making eye contact.

Within a few minutes, several others entered the courtroom through the hallway entry door, which was on Scott's right as he was now turned, facing the gallery. Perhaps they were spectators, or potential jurors who were lost and looking for the jury assembly room. Scott did not recognize any of them. Some took seats in the gallery, and some peered around the courtroom with puzzled looks and quickly left. He still did not turn his back, and the man kept the stare, still refusing to make eye contact.

In just a few minutes, Scott observed two more men coming through the entry door. Both were carrying briefcases. It was Max Gordon and James Colosimo.

Gordon seemed to have lost weight and aged quite a bit since Scott saw him at his arraignment in June. He wore a dark pinstriped suit and a silk paisley tie, but the pretentious pink handkerchief that hung loosely from his front breast pocket during the Harrison trials was missing. However, the gold Rolex on his left wrist and gold and jeweled rings on two fingers of his right hand were there as always.

Colosimo was wearing his signature white linen suit despite it being late in the season and a windy 50 degrees outside. And of course, he was trying his best to replicate the original "Diamond Jim." Paired with Gordon, they had the appearance of a gold and diamond store in a large mall. Colosimo wore diamonds on his fingers, wrist watch, cuff links, and neck tie. He was no longer wearing the braided black leather string tie with the diamond-laden clasp that he had worn during his first meeting with Scott. Instead, he wore a solid sapphire blue tie with at least a two-carat diamond stick pin. Yet, to Scott, his most striking feature was not the diamonds, but his jet black rectangular moustache that covered all of his top lip, plus at least an inch on both sides. Scott recalled the large portrait of the original "Diamond Jim" he had observed during his tour at Colosimo's. The moustache was an exact replica.

The two took seats in the red upholstered swivel chairs at the defense table. Only then did Scott turn and face away from the man in the gallery. But he didn't turn toward the defense table. He would ignore them. In any other trial with any other counsel, he would have walked over with a welcoming handshake, but this was not going to be "any other trial." This was quite unique—a shyster defending a shyster, the raw makings of a bad lawyer joke.

Richard Evans, the office investigator assigned to the case, soon arrived with enlarged copies of the photos taken by Clarence Wilborn of both Patel's and Johnson's faces, each admiring a suitcase filled with $250,000 cash. With Richard was Bob McSweeney, another DA office investigator, who would be sitting in the first row of the gallery during the trial, just behind the prosecutor's table, to assist as necessary. This was usually where Evans sat during cases he worked, but for this trial he would be a witness for the prosecution and would be excluded from the courtroom. He was present in the first Harrison robbery trial two years ago when Josh Johnson identified John Harrison as the robber at Fast Eddie's convenience store. He would provide testimony needed to prove Johnson committed perjury, which in turn was necessary to prove that Gordon committed the offense of subornation of perjury. Johnson's admission of perjury would not be sufficient to prove his perjury—that would be a single witness—but his testimony and the "corroborating evidence" provided by Richard would be sufficient. At least that was Scott's plan.

Fasi arrived at 8:45 a.m., flopped his briefcase on the table and took the chair on Scott's right. About the same time, Bill Baldwin walked in and took a seat in the gallery among several reporter friends, including several from out of town. They had all attended the three trials in this same courthouse involving John Harrison.

One half of the gallery was roped off for the eventual seating of the potential jurors, most of whom were now waiting in the Jury Assembly Room. Judge McCabe's voir dire procedure was to question an entire panel—usually thirty to thirty-six—all at once, rather than in smaller groups. The empaneled jurors would only be seated in the jury box when they were actually selected and survived any peremptory challenge. The spectator half of the gallery was rapidly filling, and by the time Judge McCabe entered there were no seats left.

There were three sharp raps on the courtroom's floor by the bailiff with the tall, banner-laden wooden staff. This, followed by the command "all rise," quickly brought the courtroom to its collective feet. Judge McCabe ordered everyone to be seated and after announcing the case for trial, inquired if counsel were prepared to proceed.

Scott stood and said, "The State is ready to proceed, Your Honor."

Colosimo stood and after introducing himself to the court, said, "The defense is ready, but we have a brief motion to make before you bring in the venire."

"Well, let's hear it," Judge McCabe responded.

"I was not present at the initial bail hearing, but I have read the transcript," said Colosimo. "At that hearing, Mr. Marino argued for what, at best, should be termed a *preposterous* bail. He argued that the acquittal, which he claims was a result of perjury by two witnesses, led to the release of Mr. John Harrison. And that as a consequence, Mr. Harrison was free to purchase a weapon and commit the felony murder of a young woman—all the fault of the alleged perjury. That, of course, is a ridiculous stretch, but it was the prosecutor's argument at the bail hearing. We expect that absurd story to be part of the prosecutor's opening statement, and they may even attempt to sneak it in on some voir dire question. Therefore, we move that the prosecution be prohibited from mentioning anything, at any time, of a murder or any consequence of the acquittal. Such evidence would be highly prejudicial; it is not relevant to the charges before the court and would indeed be grounds for a mistrial."

Scott turned his head and looked at Fasi. Fasi leaned in and whispered, "Don't fight it."

Scott had considered the issue from the time he began his preparation for the trial—and while true, the death would not have occurred but for the acquittal—it wasn't relevant to the proof of the charges now before the court. He would concede to the argument, at least in part.

"Your Honor, Mr. Colosimo's suggestion that we would, in his words, *sneak* something into evidence, is offensive. But besides that, we have no intention of introducing the evidence of the horrible consequences of this perjury—that is, in the case-in-chief. But it is clearly relevant to the sentencing phase of this trial. We ask that you withhold ruling as to its admissibility on sentencing until then."

"That appears appropriate," Judge McCabe responded. "The defense motion is granted as to the case-in-chief. At this time there is no need for an additional ruling. If there are no other motions, then we will bring in the venire and begin jury selection."

Jury selection began with Judge McCabe asking a seemingly interminable number of questions. As Fasi had said, there was little to ask after McCabe completed his questions. Neither Fasi nor Colosimo had more than twenty minutes of follow-up questions. Both Fasi and Colosimo used eight of their nine peremptory challenges and one each on the alternates. The jury selected for the case of *State of Georgia v. Maxwell E. Gordon* consisted of seven female and five male jurors, with two alternates, both female. Scott was pleased with the jury. Fasi had done his usual sterling job, but Scott was also impressed with Colosimo's use of jury strikes. As his friend Grady from Atlanta had warned him early on, he may appear weird as the "Diamond Jim" character, but he was a competent trial attorney.

The jury was sworn, and McCabe gave some basic information on what they should expect over the next few days. Then he dismissed them until the next morning.

"Does either counsel have anything for the court before we adjourn for the day?" he asked after the jury had departed. "I will not be happy if you delay the trial in the morning with motions."

Neither counsel had anything further. "We'll begin with opening statements at nine in the morning. Court is adjourned," McCabe said.

It was only 4:15 p.m. Scott was both surprised and pleased that the first day had gone so smoothly. As he picked up his briefcase to leave the courtroom, DA Office Investigator McSweeney handed him a note. "I was told this is important," McSweeney said.

Chapter Thirty-Two

Monday, November 17

Scott put his briefcase back down on the table. The note was from Richard Evans.

> Just got a call from Mike Moody, the probation officer monitoring Josh Johnson. Mike says Johnson has cut his ankle monitor. Richard.

Just what I need—a disappearing witness, Scott mused. *Not just a disappearing witness but an absolutely essential witness, with $250,000 to bet that no one will ever find him.* Scott handed the note to Fasi, grabbed his briefcase and hurried from the courtroom to find Richard.

He found him in his office, just as Richard was hanging up his phone.

"That was Moody updating me on Johnson," Richard said. "The base unit signaled that it was cut about forty-five minutes ago. Johnson's monitor was a GPS type. The reading on the base unit showed his location near the airport. Moody immediately got in contact with airport security. No sign of him there, and he's not on any manifest. Johnson's a smart guy; probably deliberately cut it near the airport as a ruse. He could be in a stolen car, rental car, Greyhound bus or just lying low in a two-bit motel off I-95. We need to get a warrant to have him arrested ASAP."

"Judge Cox has his case," Scott said. "I'll see if he's still here—he can revoke Johnson's bail and issue a warrant. Call Moody and tell him to get over here as soon as he can. The judge will probably require better proof than we can provide."

Scott took the elevator down to the judge's floor. After a quick buzz, the secretary ushered Scott into the judge's chambers. Scott explained the situation with as much detail as he knew at the time, requesting a bail revocation and arrest warrant.

"Yes, I think this calls for an emergency hearing," Judge Cox said. "Notify his attorney. Tell him to get here promptly, and if he can't, we'll go without him. I'll need the officer who was monitoring the ankle bracelet. How soon can you have him here?"

"He's on the way now. I'll try to contact Johnson's attorney. I'll call as soon as I make contact, or if I can't make contact. Thanks, Judge." Scott quickly departed.

Scott's attempts to locate Johnson's attorney were unsuccessful. And when it became clear that he could not be located, he phoned Judge Cox, who ordered the emergency bail hearing to proceed in his chambers as soon as all the available parties could be present. The hearing ended with Johnson's bail being revoked and a warrant for his arrest. Richard took on the task to immediately disseminate the warrant information to local and state law enforcement agencies.

An emergency bail revocation hearing for a missing witness was not the way Scott had hoped to end the day. The old adage that "You take your witnesses as you find them" came to mind, but with a new twist: "You take your witnesses *if* you find them." The missing witness would be a major blow but to only one charge. The subornation of perjury charge involving Patel still remained, and the two charges of influencing witnesses were solid. Conviction on any would ensure that Max Gordon remained in the criminal justice system, not as a criminal defense counsel, but as an inmate. And just the thought of that was enough to bring a smile to Scott's face. But he had a difficult decision to make before his opening statement in the morning. *Should he dismiss the charge which required the testimony of Johnson?* Right now he was willing to gamble that Johnson would be found.

Chapter Thirty-Three

Tuesday, November 18

"May it please the court and members of the jury . . ." Scott began his opening statement to the jury at 9:15 a.m. in the packed courtroom.

He was standing in front of the jury, ten to twelve feet away, and speaking without notes. Unlike some judges who required counsel to address the jury from a lectern, Judge McCabe had no such rule, and Scott was taking full advantage of the open space. He had a strong, persuasive voice, and the opening statement allowed him to use it. He had worked hard on its preparation over the past several weeks. The facts of the case and the elements of proof seemed simple enough to him, but for a jury hearing the facts for the first time, it could be a bit overwhelming. He would have to be careful with the structure and convincing in its delivery. And now it was a bit complicated with the disappearance of Johnson. He had wrestled with his initial decision not to dismiss the charge that required Johnson's testimony. He had discussed it with Fasi, and Fasi advised him that there was no right or wrong decision in such circumstances, but to "go with your gut." Scott was betting that Johnson would be found, arrested, and brought to the courthouse in time to testify, so he made the decision to keep the charge before the court. Johnson's name as a potential witness had come up during voir dire, and he considered how that should be handled in the opening statement. He decided it best not to mention Johnson at all in the opening. Colosimo, in his closing argument, would surely jump on anything mentioned in the opening and not proved.

"In this same courtroom in September of last year, two men stood just a few feet from where you are now," he continued. "They placed a hand on a Bible and took an oath 'to tell the truth, the whole truth, and nothing but the truth.' They were witnesses in a felony trial, a robbery that occurred here in Savannah. But neither man had any intention of telling the truth. They arrived in court with just the opposite intention—to tell a lie and nothing but a lie. And as you will find out, they did exactly that. And by doing so, both committed the offense of perjury.

"But why? That's a question which will be answered with the evidence that you will hear today and tomorrow. But let me give you the short version of the answer. *Money.* Lots of money. In fact $250,000 to each of these two witnesses. For their lies. And who provided that money? You will learn that the money came from a man seated right now in this very courtroom."

Scott turned and looked at Max Gordon. Then he walked to the defense table and stood next to Gordon. "And *that man* is seated right here," Scott said, pointing directly at Gordon, who was seated with his arms folded, his face fixed in a grimace, his eyes focused on the floor in front of him. "He is Maxwell E. Gordon, and he is the defendant in this case."

Scott returned to his original position in front of the jury, and continued. "The evidence will show that money, lots of it, is the reason these men lied, and the defendant is the person who provided it. But then the question remains, *why* did the defendant provide $250,000 to these two men? We know the motive of the two men to lie was the payoff of $250,000 cash, but what was the motive of the defendant for providing this payoff? We will provide that answer also with testimony over the next day or two. But I have a shorthand answer to that question now.

"You see, members of the jury, the defendant . . ." Scott stopped, turned and again pointed at Gordon. ". . . is an attorney, and he was representing a client by the name of John Harrison, charged with the crime of robbery. This was a retrial. The first trial resulted in a conviction and John Harrison was sentenced to ten years confinement in the state prison. But that conviction was overturned on appeal, so John Harrison was to be tried again for the robbery. It so happens that John Harrison's father, David Harrison, was a very wealthy man, and as a father, he did not wish to see his son convicted of robbery again. He was able and willing to provide substantial funds for his son's defense, and he hired the defendant.

"Unfortunately for the defense, there were two eyewitnesses to the robbery. Both had identified the defendant during the first trial as the man they saw holding a gun during the robbery. And they were the only eyewitnesses."

Scott stopped, turned to look at Gordon, and then pointed once more at him as he continued. "So this defendant realized that he could obtain an acquittal if he could buy these two witnesses. And that he did, for $250,000 each. Funds provided by David Harrison and put into play by the defendant sitting now in this courtroom, right over there at the defense table. We don't know if David Harrison was involved in the defendant's plan or even knew of the defendant's plan, and we don't need to know. What we *know* is that it was the defendant who executed the plan with the help of his co-counsel, an attorney by the name of Clarence Wilborn, from Macon, Georgia.

"Clarence Wilborn has admitted his involvement in this scheme. Wilborn was also involved in a major drug ring in Macon and Atlanta. It was through the drug connection that Gordon was able to launder, that is, *convert*, David Harrison's payments to Gordon into actual paper money for the payoff. Wilborn will testify that Gordon hired an agent to negotiate the deal with the two witnesses, and at Gordon's direction, Wilborn traveled by automobile to deliver the cash. One witness was living in Colorado, and one by the name of Vijay Patel, was living right here in Savannah. Wilborn will identify photos he took of the witnesses, each smiling as they viewed their newly delivered suitcase filled with $250,000 cash.

"The payoff worked. Each witness, despite their oath to tell the truth, deliberately lied." Scott once again pointed at Gordon. "John Harrison was seated at that very table where this defendant is seated. And both witnesses, when asked to identify the man with the gun, lied by saying it was not the defendant, John Harrison. The result? John Harrison was acquitted."

Scott used most of the remainder of his opening to introduce the jury to the testimony that would be coming from Carl DeBickero, who would be his first witness. He did not attempt to explain "subornation of perjury," a term surely unfamiliar to many on the jury. The elements of proof required would be explained later when the judge gave the jury its instructions, and Scott would link the evidence to the required proof during closing argument. He also did not explain "the two-witness rule," as this was a rule that benefitted only the defense. Perhaps Colosimo would bring it up in his opening statement, but Scott saw no reason to even mention it until closing arguments.

Scott looked at the courtroom clock. He had been speaking for only twenty minutes, but it was time to wrap it up. "Members of the jury, yesterday you were informed of the charges against this defendant, and afterwards you took an oath, a solemn oath to render a true verdict on those charges according to the evidence. When this trial is concluded, I'm confident you'll honor that oath by your verdict: a verdict of guilty to each and every charge. Thank you."

"Does the defense wish to make an opening statement now or reserve it for later?" asked Judge McCabe.

Colosimo stood and responded, "We'll reserve it."

Scott noted that from the beginning of the trial, Colosimo had never used the words, "Your Honor" when addressing the judge. He wondered if this was deliberate. He was surprised that Colosimo chose not to make his opening statement now. Most defense counsel made their opening at the beginning of the trial to counter or at least blunt the prosecutor's presentation. By waiting, the jury heard only one side, and it became harder to dislodge the negative impression of the defendant that remains unchallenged until the defense case. But there were occasions when waiting was the best option, and Scott feared this might be one of them, as it was preventing him from having any knowledge of what the defense in the case would be. Here he was prosecuting a case with a criminal defense attorney defending a criminal defense attorney. He had no idea of what schemes those two could produce, especially when assisted by two disbarred and totally corrupt lawyers who had already displayed their cunning skills on the street in front of the Henry Grady Inn.

"The prosecution may call its first witness," the judge said.

Scott called Carl DeBickero. Carl recounted how the case unfolded from the beginning, with the arrest of Clarence Wilborn and his offer to cooperate in exchange for sentencing benefits. He testified to the arrest of Patel, Patel turning over to him the $250,000 cash he had received from Wilborn, and his arrest of the defendant, Max Gordon. His direct testimony lasted slightly less than an hour.

Colosimo stood to begin his cross-examination. He pressed the sides of his head, apparently to smooth down any protruding hair, then did the same to the black, rectangular moustache that extended halfway across his face. He walked to the lectern and placed some notes on it. He then took a few steps to the left. He began his cross-examination without any written notes or papers.

"I listened carefully to your testimony, Mr. DeBickero. You did not testify to any interview with Mr. David Harrison, whose money you claim financed this alleged perjury. Did you interview Mr. Harrison?"

"No, I did not," Carl responded.

"And that was because Mr. Harrison had a severe stroke and was unable to communicate, isn't that right?"

"Yes."

"In fact, last month Mr. Harrison succumbed to that stroke, correct?"

"That is correct."

"So none of the information you have provided concerning the source of these funds came from Mr. Harrison, did it?"

"No, it did not," Carl responded.

"I listened carefully for testimony linking these payoff funds to Mr. Gordon. What I heard was that any link to Mr. Gordon was provided entirely by what Clarence Wilborn told you. Did I miss something, Mr. DeBickero?"

Carl paused for a long while before responding. "No, that's correct. It was Wilborn who provided the information."

"And I listened for the name of the individual who Mr. Gordon allegedly hired—the man who allegedly contacted the witnesses to fix the payments for their alleged perjury. I did not hear a name. Did I miss that also, Mr. DeBickero?"

Carl paused and tightened his lips before responding. "No, we were not able to learn his name. Wilborn never learned his name. He said—"

Colosimo quickly cut him off. "Just answer my question. You do not know the name of this so-called 'agent' of Mr. Gordon, do you?"

"No, sir."

"You have been the assigned senior GBI agent for this investigation since it began over a year ago, correct?"

"Yes."

"And finding that agent of Mr. Gordon has been an important task, correct?"

"Yes."

"You had others in the Georgia Bureau of Investigation to assist you?"

"That is true."

"And you and others have spent many days and hours trying to identify this person?"

"Yes."

"How much of that time was spent trying to determine if it was indeed Mr. Gordon who hired that man, or if perhaps it was Mr. Wilborn who hired this fixer?"

"Our time has been spent trying to find the person, regardless of who hired him."

"Would it have made any difference to your investigation if you found that it was Clarence Wilborn who hired him and not Mr. Gordon?"

"Not really. Wilborn worked under the direction of Mr. Gordon. Mr. Wilborn was hired because Mr. Gordon was not a member of the Georgia Bar. Wilborn was his sponsor for this trial. And of course, Wilborn has also been charged. He is jointly responsible for these crimes along with the defendant."

"During your investigation did you consider that Mr. Wilborn may have undertaken these crimes himself, without the direction or concurrence of Mr. Gordon?"

"As I said, Wilborn worked under the direction of Gordon. Gordon was the lead attorney in charge of the defense of John Harrison."

"That was not the question. I'm sure the jury would appreciate you answering the question. Shall I repeat it?"

"No, I recall the question. We conducted a thorough investigation and saw no reason to take the focus off the prime suspect, Max Gordon."

"You apparently aren't going to answer the question, so let me answer it for you. You have been conducting this investigation for over a year, and not once, *not once*, have you ever considered that the alleged perjured testimony resulted from a scheme by Clarence Wilborn alone, without the concurrence or even knowledge of Mr. Gordon." Colosimo turned, walked over to the lectern and picked up the papers he had left there, then added, "I have no further questions of this *so-called* witness."

Scott rose from his chair. "Your Honor, I object to that spurious comment by Mr. Colosimo. Such comments are uncalled for."

"This appears to be an appropriate time for our morning break," Judge McCabe said. "Bailiff, please escort the jury out. Counsel, please remain."

When the jury had departed and counsel once more were seated, Judge McCabe sat forward in his chair and looked sternly at Colosimo. "Let me be perfectly clear, Mr. Colosimo. Such insulting remarks to witnesses will not go unnoticed by the court or the jury. It will not help you with the jury, and it will not be tolerated by the court. This is not a ball game where you get three strikes. In this court, you get one strike. Two, and you'll be held in contempt, or worse. This time I will just consider it an isolated lapse, but I suggest you don't test me. Have I made myself clear?"

Colosimo stood, looking down and refusing to make eye contact with the judge. "You have made yourself quite clear," he replied. "And I apologize for the remark. It will not happen again."

"We will be in recess until eleven," the judge responded. "Redirect examination may be conducted then."

Scott and Fasi remained in the courtroom to discuss the significance of Colosimo's cross-examination. He had not made an opening statement that might have alerted them to Gordon's defense, so this was the first hint of what the defense would be: *It was quite simple. Clarence Wilborn alone planned and executed the scheme, all without the assistance or knowledge of Gordon.* But it did not come as an actual surprise. They had considered all likely defenses, and some highly unlikely—such as entrapment—but with the evidence available to the prosecution, none seemed to have any reasonable chance of success, including the one suggested by Colosimo's recent cross-examination. There was no evidence that Wilborn was responsible, and they could conceive of no motive for such independent action on his part. David Harrison had hired Gordon to defend his son, and Wilborn entered the defense merely because Gordon was not a member of the Georgia Bar and thus needed a sponsor. Wilborn would have had to secretly obtain the funds needed for the pay-off from David Harrison, and there was no evidence that the two had even met. Scott could conceive of no way the defense could pull it off. But he also saw two experienced criminal defense attorneys seated at the other table, both with sharp and cunning minds. Anything was possible.

When the jury was back in and Scott had his opportunity for redirect examination, he had a single question for DeBickero.

"During this lengthy investigation of the charges against the defendant, did you find any evidence—any evidence at all—to suggest that these crimes were the independent action of Clarence Wilborn, acting without the concurrence or knowledge of the defendant?"

"I did not," Carl responded.

There was no recross-examination and Scott called his next witness, Clarence Wilborn. The initial questions pertained to his bio—residence, education and law practice. Scott also asked if he had ever been disciplined by the Georgia Bar, which he admitted, explaining his law license was suspended for a year for commingling client funds. Scott had a special reason for this question, and he expected it to come up again later in the trial. After the biographical questions, the questioning turned to when and how Wilborn was brought into the case, his duties, assignments, and salary. He testified that he made at least five trips to Chicago to meet with Gordon, where they discussed all the possible defenses, both the legal ones and the illegal one that they finally agreed upon—to pay the two witnesses to lie at the trial. He told of his own involvement in an illegal drug cartel that was headquartered in Atlanta and of his introduction of Gordon to some of the higher operatives. These cartel agents were experts at moving their drug money through multiple bank accounts, including some off-shore accounts, so that the money was washed clean. A reverse laundering would occur with Senator David Harrison's checks, which would start out clean and end up dirty. But the process was similar. He testified that after he introduced Gordon to the cartel agents, Gordon handled all the details. Gordon hired the man who negotiated the $250,000 deals with the two witnesses. He never met the man nor learned of his identity. When the arrangements were complete, he went to the cartel headquarters in Atlanta, picked up the cash in two suitcases and drove to Colorado and Savannah to deliver them. Wilborn authenticated the photos he took of both Patel and Johnson with smiles on their faces as they ogled the money. These were photos taken at the direction of Gordon to ensure that the recipients of the cash were locked into the scheme. Finally he told of his arrest on drug charges and his offer to assist in this case in exchange for a more favorable sentence.

Wilborn's direct examination was completed at 3:10 p.m., after being interrupted by the lunch break. There were only a couple of objections by Colosimo to his testimony, which surprised Scott. He had anticipated Colosimo being a fully irascible and confrontational trial attorney. Scott had occasionally looked over at the defense table to observe Gordon. Gordon sat quietly, with a somber, disinterested look on his face. Scott wondered if this was the calm before the storm. Judge McCabe called a court recess until 3:30 p.m., when the cross-examination would begin.

During the recess, Scott sent McSweeney to check if there was anything new in the hunt for Josh Johnson. There was not. So far there had been no sightings or tips, and Scott was beginning to lose hope that Johnson would be located in time to testify. McSweeney also reported that Patel was still in one of the small witness waiting rooms. He appeared quite nervous, as would be expected, but

Luke Schaub, his attorney, was checking in with him frequently. Unless Johnson was located, Patel would be his only witness on the subornation of perjury indictment. However, conviction on either one of those two charges, along with the two charges of influencing witnesses, would ensure that Gordon was put away for many years and would lose his law license. To Scott, making sure he lost his law license and thus his ability to continue to spread his corruption within the criminal justice system was even more important than any prison time he might serve.

Colosimo began his cross examination by testing Wilborn on many minor details, hoping to show inconsistencies and discrepancies in his testimony. This was expected and was generally ineffective, as Scott had schooled Wilborn during many witness preparation sessions over the past few weeks on what to expect. He held up well, providing very little that would benefit the defense. But Scott knew it would be different when Colosimo zeroed in on his pretrial agreements for the charges in this case and his drug charges in Atlanta.

"So you were a part of a major drug cartel working out of Atlanta?"

"Yes."

"Your cartel covered quite a bit of territory—north Georgia and parts of Alabama, Tennessee and South Carolina?"

"Yes, sir."

"Selling marijuana, cocaine, and any drug you could get your hands on to make a profit, right?"

"Yes."

"And you got caught?"

"Yes."

"By the feds?"

"Yes, sir."

"They caught you with 300 grams, cocaine mixture, and charged you with trafficking, correct?"

"Yes, that's right."

"And the case was solid, wasn't it? They had you cold, isn't that correct?"

"I believe so."

"Now you've told the jury you are an attorney. You are, or were, a criminal defense attorney?"

"That's right."

"Defended clients facing drug charges?"

"Yes."

"Sort of a specialty of your practice—drug offenses, right?"

"I suppose you could say that."

"Well, I think *you* were saying that on your law firm's website. You had a federal drug trafficking penalty chart right on your website, didn't you?"

"Yes."

"In fact, that was your major practice, defending drug offenses?"

"I defended quite a few, not sure I would call it my major practice."

"Well, I guess not. Apparently your major practice was *dealing* in drugs. That's how you made most of your money, wasn't it? Drug dealing?"

Wilborn did not answer. He looked down at the floor in front of him and then to Scott. But Scott could not help him. The only objection that he could think of was relevancy, and to make that objection would only underscore the fact that he was a drug dealer, which the jury already knew.

"So when the feds arrested you, you knew you were in big trouble. Really big trouble, right?"

"Yes."

"I want you to turn to the jury, Mr. Wilborn, and tell them just how *big* that trouble was. Tell the jury just what was the maximum penalty you were facing, caught trafficking with that 300 grams of cocaine."

"Sentence of ten years."

"Sentence of ten years? Now Mr. Wilborn. That's a deceptive statement, isn't it? You know that ten years is the *minimum* sentence for that amount of cocaine. What's the maximum sentence you were facing?"

"I think it's life."

"You don't *think* it, you *know* it, don't you, Mr. Wilborn?"

"I suppose so."

"*Suppose* so? You *know* so. In fact, you had 'life' written in bold letters on that drug trafficking penalty chart right on your website. Isn't that true?"

Scott realized that all his coaching and preparation was for naught. Why would an experienced attorney respond this way? One weasel response leads to another, and all the time the jury is sizing up the credibility of Scott's chief witness.

"Ok . . . Ok. It's life. Max sentence is life."

"So facing a possible sentence of life in prison, you cut a deal, right?"

"I was approached with a deal."

"*Approached* with a deal. OK. That was from that GBI agent, right?"

"Yes."

"And it was quite a deal, wasn't it? Got the feds to turn the case over to the state for prosecution. Instead of facing a *minimum* of ten years confinement and a maximum of life imprisonment, you got a deal for a *maximum* of ten. Quite a deal wasn't it, Mr. Wilborn?"

Wilborn did not respond.

"All you had to do was testify against Mr. Gordon, right?"

"Testify truthfully," added Wilborn.

"I'm glad you mentioned that, Mr. Wilborn. Your so-called truthful testimony had to correspond with what the prosecutor is expecting from you now, correct?"

"I don't know what the prosecutor is expecting."

"Oh, you don't?" Colosimo walked to the defense table, picked up a document, and looked at Judge McCabe. "May I approach the witness?" he said.

Scott noted again that Colosimo never used the term, "Your Honor," which most attorneys used frequently as a term of respect when addressing a trial judge. He also noted that his star witness's credibility was about to take another beating, assuming he had any credibility left.

After the judge granted the request, Colosimo approached the witness with the document he had retrieved from the table. "In fact Mr. Wilborn," he continued, "I believe I have your statement right here." He briefly showed the document to Wilborn. "Is this your statement?"

Another weak response of "yes."

"At the bottom of this three-page, typed statement, it reads, 'The above is a true statement, and if my pretrial agreement is approved, I agree to testify truthfully in substance as written above. Signed, Clarence Wilborn.'" Colosimo handed the statement to Wilborn.

"Did I read that correctly, Mr. Wilborn?"

Wilborn did not respond and looked over at Scott. They made eye contact, and Wilborn must have seen the exasperation—or perhaps anger—in Scott's eyes. He responded immediately with an almost inaudible "yes."

"You didn't prepare this document, did you, Mr. Wilborn?"

"No."

"In fact, it was prepared by that GBI agent who bailed you out of the awful predicament you were in, correct?"

"Yes."

"This was your ticket out of a possible sentence to life imprisonment in a federal penitentiary, right?"

Wilborn stared at Colosimo but did not respond.

"Yes, your ticket out. Drafted by the GBI, typed by the GBI and thrust in front of you to sign, right?"

Wilborn still did not respond.

"The jury is waiting for a response, Mr. Wilborn. It was your ticket out. Drafted by the GBI, typed by the GBI and thrust in front of you with a pen to sign, right?"

Another pause, then a barely audible, "yes."

And so the attack on his credibility went for another ten to fifteen minutes. And then the questions began that would introduce the jury to the essence of Gordon's defense.

"And at no time did you tell the GBI agent of what really happened, did you Mr. Wilborn?"

Wilborn looked confused. There was a long pause before he answered. Finally, "I don't understand your question."

"Oh, I think you do, Mr. Wilborn. But we'll get back to that. Wasn't it last August that you were asked by Mr. Gordon to assist with the Harrison case?"

"Yes."

"He needed you, or someone with a Georgia Bar license, to sponsor him?"

"That's correct."

"And you accepted it because the pay was going to be quite substantial, correct?"

"Well, I accepted it."

"You knew the defendant was the son of one of the richest men in Georgia, didn't you?"

"According to Mr. Gordon, yes."

"And you knew he would provide whatever amount of money was necessary to defend his son?"

"I don't know. But that's what Mr. Gordon said, yes."

"Now tell me if this is what you recall. Listen carefully. After you agreed to enter the case and accept the assignment as sponsor for Mr. Gordon, you flew to Chicago, met with him in his office in midafternoon to discuss the case. And he explained all the evidence the prosecution would be presenting at trial. Is that what you recall?"

"Yes, I recall that."

"You would be staying overnight in Chicago, so he invited you to join him for dinner, right?"

"Yes."

"Seven o'clock, at Gallucci's, a short walk from your hotel. Is that how you recall it?"

"I think so."

Scott wondered where Colosimo was going with this line of questions. Again he thought of objecting on relevancy grounds but decided to wait for the time being.

"You got there first, had them seat you in a nice quiet corner, ordered a drink and there you waited for Mr. Gordon, correct?"

Wilborn paused for a long moment before responding. "Yes."

"He found you and ordered a drink also, and the two of you ordered dinner, right?"

"Of course. That's what we were there for."

"That's what *Mr. Gordon* was there for. But you had something else in mind, didn't you?"

Wilborn frowned but did not immediately answer.

"It was during that dinner at Gallucci's restaurant that you suggested to Mr. Gordon that the best way to defend the case was to buy off the two witnesses, isn't that correct, Mr. Wilborn?"

So this is where he was heading, thought Scott. *Setting up a time and place—a quiet corner of a nice Italian restaurant to bring a touch of drama to this bizarre defense. Quite clever. Colosimo surely knows that this accusation will be denied by the witness. But what is important is that the seed for the defense has been presented in a realistic way to the jury. The jury wants time, place, and circumstances for all evidence. They have it now.*

"That's not true," replied Wilborn.

"Mr. Gordon refused to discuss this plan of yours, didn't he, Mr. Wilborn?"

"There was nothing to discuss."

"So you decided you would carry it out yourself, isn't that true?"

"No, that's not true."

"And you paid a personal visit to Mr. Harrison, explained your plan, and he provided the funds. And you carried out this crime alone, without the consent or knowledge of Mr. Gordon. Isn't this also true, Mr. Wilborn?"

Several evidentiary objections came to mind, but Scott decided it best to let Colosimo proceed with this absurd defense. No juror would believe such fantasy. Colosimo would dig a hole and bury both himself and his client.

When Colosimo ended his cross-examination, Scott had just a few questions on redirect examination.

"Did you fully explain to the GBI agent, Carl DeBickero, your involvement in these crimes before he prepared the document that you signed?" Scott had noted that Colosimo had refused to refer to Carl by name, always calling him "that GBI agent." Scott would be sure to refer to him by his name. He followed that question with, "Was there anything in the statement Carl DeBickero prepared that you had not already described as being true?"

"No."

"The defense counsel asked you a number of questions suggesting that you recommended this crime to the defendant at a restaurant in Chicago, that he refused, and you then executed it yourself without his knowledge. How much of that was true?"

"None, except we did have dinner together at a Chicago restaurant the first time I met with the defendant, but the payoff scheme was not discussed. That was not discussed until the following week, during our second meeting. By then it was all planned out by the defendant. I'm not saying I didn't agree. I did. But it was a mutual agreement. My main contribution was the delivery of the cash. I certainly did not contact Mr. Harrison myself. That would have been foolish. I never even met the man."

Scott had no additional questions and Wilborn was excused as a witness. It was now 5:15 p.m. and Judge McCabe recessed the court until 9:00 a.m. the following morning. Scott looked back at the gallery. It had been filled to capacity, but the crowd was hastily departing. He saw the man he had seen earlier—the man he recognized as a member of Colosimo's staff. He was approaching the defense table, along with another man who Scott thought he also recognized from Colosimo's web page. He wasn't sure, but it looked like the other disbarred attorney who Colosimo proudly claimed as a "staff member." The two "staff members" and Colosimo, along with the defendant, were soon joined in what appeared to be a serious discussion. Scott watched while gathering his notes, then closed his briefcase and left the courtroom. He was anxious to return to his office and check if Johnson had been located.

He received the news from Richard Evans. No sight or sound of Johnson. He immediately called Luke Schaub.

"Johnson's still missing, so I'll be calling Patel as the first witness in the morning. I'd like to have a brief chat with him first. Please have him there no later than eight-thirty."

"Sure, we'll be there."

Chapter Thirty-Four

Wednesday, November 19

Scott drove to the Chatham County Courthouse in a heavy early morning rain, still hoping for news of Johnson's arrest. If so, Patel would still be his first witness, and Fasi could prepare Johnson for his testimony, which would be next.

Anxious to start preparing Patel for his testimony, Scott hurried to the witness waiting room. It was 8:30 a.m., the time agreed upon, but no one was there. Perhaps, he thought, Luke and Patel are waiting in the courtroom. But as he entered the courtroom, he saw that it was almost vacant—just a bailiff and a couple of early risers who wanted to make sure they had a seat. He sat in a chair at his table and waited. Scott did not expect Fasi until shortly before 9:00 a.m.

Soon, Luke Schaub entered the courtroom—alone. His expression was grim, and he was slowly shaking his head as he approached. He sank hard into one of the upholstered chairs next to Scott, who knew immediately, *this is not good.*

"I stopped by Patel's store, but he wasn't there. I was to pick him up at eight, grab a cup of coffee, and come on over. His cashier said she hadn't seen him; he hadn't been in. I waited a while, then decided he must have come straight over here. Nope. Not in the witness room, and no one seems to have seen him. Makes no sense; he wanted to get this over."

"Yes, and I cut him a good deal and let him out on bail," Scott said, before biting his lip and staring off in space. He was silent, deep in thought, then said quietly to no one in particular, "I know, no good deed . . ." He struck the table hard with his fist and turned to Luke. "You don't suppose those two depraved bastards bought off these two witnesses *again*. First to *lie* and now to *disappear*? What's the saying, 'Fool me once, shame on you; but fool me twice . . . '? Well, it's on me now. I'll have to take the fall for this one. They had already proven they could be bought. I should have kept them both locked up. Yes, I screwed up royally."

"I don't believe Patel was bought, Scott. I gave him strict instructions to speak with no one about this case and to call me immediately if anyone attempted to speak with him about it. I think he understood. He knew he was facing a long prison sentence in the state pen, and he knew you gave him a good deal. I'm at a loss to understand why he's missing, but I don't believe he was bought, as you call it, again. I'm going back to my office. Have someone call me if he shows, and I'll call you if I locate him." Luke got up from his chair and left the courtroom.

At that time, Scott saw Fasi coming through the entrance, along with Bob McSweeney. *Maybe they would have good news.*

They didn't. "Still no sign of Johnson," McSweeney said. "I just spoke with Richard. He's been in contact with every county and state agency that may have any information, and there is none."

"Well, I have no more witnesses now." Scott folded his arms across his chest and took a deep breath. He was visibly upset and frustrated. And he felt a deep personal failure. "Any suggestions, Joe?"

"Scott, sometimes these things happen, no matter how much time and effort you put into the planning," Joe replied. "It's not a great defeat. You still have the witness influencing charges. That will be enough to send him to prison. And I know one of your primary concerns is also to get him disbarred, and a conviction on either of the remaining charges will surely do that. Of course, you'll get a motion for a judgment of acquittal on the subornation charges, so just accept it and get ready for whatever the defense tries to throw at the jury. You are going to win this case."

Judge McCabe entered, soon followed by the jury. Scott dreaded to hear the words he knew the judge would be saying next.

"Call your next witness."

Scott stood. "Your Honor, the State rests."

This announcement came as a big surprise to the newsmen and spectators in the gallery, prompting a mild but disruptive frenzy. The disturbance was quickly quelled by three sharp raps of Judge McCabe's gavel. He instructed the bailiff to take the jury out—not because of the commotion in the gallery but because he knew that the defense would now be making a motion.

As soon as the jury was removed, Colosimo stood. "The defense moves for a directed verdict of acquittal on all charges."

Scott had expected such a motion on the subornation of perjury charges. Not only had he failed to prove perjury with two witnesses, he had produced *no* witnesses. But he was momentary stunned by the motion directed at *all charges*. The witness influencing charges did not require two witnesses. He was sure the unrebutted testimony of Wilborn concerning the payments to the two witnesses to lie was sufficient under the law. Nevertheless, the motion alarmed him.

Colosimo began his argument on the motion by noting the absence of any witnesses to perjury. Then he lashed out at the credibility of Wilborn, arguing that "no reasonable juror could believe him" and thus none of the charges were proved.

Scott rose to respond. "Your Honor, we do not contest the defense motion as it relates to the charges of subornation of perjury. Our witnesses have disappeared. But we have presented sufficient evidence on each and every element of the charges of influencing the two witnesses. Whether Clarence Wilborn is believable is for the jury to determine."

Judge McCabe quickly ruled. "The motion with regard to both charges alleging subornation of perjury is granted. The motion as it relates to charges of influencing a witness is denied. Bailiff, please bring in the jury. We will begin with the defense case."

Chapter Thirty-Five

Wednesday, November 19

When the jury was back in the courtroom and seated, Judge McCabe looked toward the defense table. "Mr. Colosimo, you waived your opening. Do you wish to make an opening statement now?"

"No, I'm sure this jury understands what this case is about. I'll call my first, and my only witness, Mr. Maxwell Gordon," Colosimo responded, emphasizing *only*.

Scott was surprised that Colosimo did not take the opportunity to address the jury with an opening statement as invited by the judge. But he also realized that Colosimo was probably right—the jury did indeed know what the case was about. There was no surprise that Gordon would be the only witness, because the defense had not provided a witness list, a requirement if they planned to call any witnesses other than the defendant. Emphasizing that the only defense witness would be Gordon seemed to be something Colosimo was proud of—sort of "that's all we need." Both Scott and Fasi thought this to be a strange strategy. They knew Gordon could not produce a *truthful* witness to support his claim that Wilborn, and only Wilborn, was responsible for the crimes, but that should present no hindrance to Gordon—*lying* witnesses was his specialty.

They had expected a long list of such witnesses, as well as a list of witnesses they had no intention of calling, a common defense ruse used to send prosecutors off on a futile hunt for evidence, wasting precious trial preparation time. They had also anticipated a list of supposedly distinguished citizens who would testify to his "sterling character." But the defense sent no list of any kind. Apparently the defense was convinced that its simple strategy of pitting Gordon's sworn testimony against the testimony of a fully discredited Clarence Wilborn would be more compelling.

Colosimo began by asking a number of personal questions, establishing that Gordon was an attorney, a member of three different state bar associations, admitted to practice before the United States Supreme Court and numerous other federal courts. He earned a "national reputation for success"—his description—and was "eminently known for taking on tough cases and unpopular causes, and winning"—also his description. Scott could have objected to this inadmissible bolstering, but he thought it best to let the pompous clown bore the jury with such self-aggrandizement.

Then the questioning moved to the circumstances surrounding the charges in this case. Gordon testified that he had been asked by Senator Harrison, "a longtime and special friend"—again his words—to defend his son, who was facing a serious charge—robbery. He was convicted, but the verdict was reversed on appeal. Again he was asked by Senator Harrison to defend his son and again he accepted. This time his son was acquitted.

"What did that acquittal have to do with the charges in this case?" Colosimo asked.

"Everything," answered Gordon. "The trial was covered by TV and news media throughout Georgia. There was also national media present. The Chatham County District Attorney was extremely embarrassed that he charged the son of one of Georgia's most revered politicians and lost. The DA's future campaign for governor was severely hurt."

Scott and Fasi sent puzzled looks to each other. Josh Magidson had never even hinted at running for governor or any other state office. The jury was composed of Savannah citizens, and they would have heard nothing, not even a rumor, of such aspirations on the part of the district attorney. *Surely the jury would see this for what it was, pure nonsense*, Scott thought. Fasi's face showed a slight smile.

"And how did that impact this case, Mr. Gordon?" Colosimo asked.

"The DA was angry and sought revenge."

Scott was up immediately. "Objection, Your Honor! That is pure speculation. I move to strike it."

"Yes, the objection is sustained. The jury must disregard the witness's last answer."

Scott got what he wanted, but he knew that Colosimo also got what he wanted. He had suggested a motive for the charges against his client.

"Well, let me put it this way, Mr. Gordon—what action did the district attorney take?"

"He brought these charges against me, so that now I'm in a courtroom, but not as a defense counsel, where I have served successfully and honorably for thirty years. I am here as a defendant facing false charges."

"Tell the jury the real facts about these charges, as you know them."

"If the witnesses lied, I know nothing about it. If the witnesses were paid to lie, as the prosecution claims, I know nothing of it. Clarence Wilborn says he delivered $250,000 to each witness. That may be true, but I have no knowledge of it except his testimony. There has been no other evidence connecting me to this offense except his statement to the GBI agent and his testimony in court yesterday. The investigation of the charges against me revealed nothing except what was contained in Clarence Wilborn's lies. It was convenient for this investigation to focus on me. That's what the district attorney wanted. And that's what Mr. Marino wanted—they wanted the GBI to serve me up on a platter, and that's what happened."

Scott considered objecting. It was pure speculation for the witness to testify what the district attorney "wanted," or what Scott "wanted." That may be an argument for Colosimo to try to work into his closing argument, but this witness had no personal knowledge of it. Scott had a valid objection, but he decided not to object. Right or wrong, he felt such an objection put him in a defensive mode. He, as well as Colosimo, could address this in the closing, and Scott felt he would prevail.

For the next fifteen minutes, the defendant answered Colosimo's questions with essentially the same answers: the money for the payoff was obtained by Wilborn without Gordon's knowledge; it was delivered to the witnesses without his knowledge; and he had no knowledge of the payoff or the perjured testimony until he was arrested.

When Colosimo completed his direct exam, Judge McCabe ordered a twenty minute recess. Scott was pleased to have this time to consider his options. One was to merely say, "No questions." The jury could see the lameness of the defense case. There was no real issue of whether the witnesses received the payoff as claimed by Wilborn. He had photos of both Patel and Johnson admiring their cash. And DeBickero had confiscated Patel's suitcase still filled with all the cash he had received. No, there was no question that the witnesses had received the cash and for no other plausible reason except to lie at the trial. So why would Wilborn do this except for that purpose? And no one could believe that Wilborn would take it upon himself to make the payoff without directions from Gordon. After all, his main role in the case was to provide the needed Georgia Bar member sponsorship for Gordon.

Yes, Scott could merely say, "No questions," but he believed every juror would expect some cross-examination after a defendant took the witness stand and denied involvement, even if the denial was utterly incredible. So Scott began with a few questions about a link between Wilborn and Senator Harrison. *No, Wilborn had never gone with him to the Senator's office. No, he had never introduced the two. No, he could not provide any evidence that linked Wilborn to Senator Harrison in any way.*

Then Scott moved on to questions of Gordon's relationship to Wilborn—when and how they first met.

"I am not a member of the Georgia Bar, so I needed someone with a Georgia Bar license to sponsor me for the trial. I called an attorney friend in Atlanta and he recommended Clarence Wilborn," Gordon testified.

"Your friend didn't volunteer to sponsor you?" Scott asked.

"No, he was too busy with his own practice," Gordon responded.

"What were the special traits of Clarence Wilborn that prompted that recommendation?"

"I don't know. I trusted my friend. I've known him for years."

"You didn't have to tell him. He knew the type of attorney you wanted, didn't he?"

"I don't understand your question," Gordon responded.

"You were in this courtroom when Clarence Wilborn testified. He testified he had been suspended from practice for a year for misconduct, commingling funds. And he was into drugs— buying and selling. A major drug cartel. That's a man you can do business with—the man you wanted on your team, right?"

"I had no knowledge of that, none at all," Gordon replied.

"You are telling this jury that you hired an attorney without vetting him at all? You know you could have checked him out, don't you?"

"You expect me to be clairvoyant? I'm to know that an attorney is going to commit a crime?"

"No, not that an attorney is *going* to commit a crime but to check if he has *already* committed a crime. He testified yesterday that he had his license suspended for a year for misconduct. You could have checked that, right?"

"I checked to see if he had a Georgia Bar license. The only thing I needed was his license."

"Of course. Where did you check?"

"The Georgia Bar website. It lists all the Georgia Bar members. He was listed."

"And it also states whether the member has ever been disciplined, right?"

Gordon did not respond so Scott continued.

"Right there on the website below the name, in bold red letters, it states whether the member has, or does not have, any public disciplinary history, doesn't it?"

Gordon twisted in his seat but again did not respond immediately, so Scott pressed on.

"When you saw that entry in red for Clarence Wilborn, it confirmed what your friend had already told you, didn't it? That Clarence Wilborn was just the corrupt-type associate you wanted. Just the man you needed for the job, right?"

"Absolutely not! And I certainly had no idea he would come to this courtroom with his lies, just as I had no idea those two witnesses would lie."

"I'm glad you mentioned that, Mr. Gordon, that you had no idea those two witnesses would lie. In fact, you knew in advance they would lie, didn't you?"

"I've answered that. The answer is 'no.' And it will be 'no' the next time you ask that question."

"Do you recall that moment in the trial when the witness, Johnson, said he couldn't identify the defendant as the robber?"

"I do, of course."

"You saw the astonishment on the face of Mr. Cox, the prosecutor, didn't you?" Scott asked.

"Yes, but I would call it pure shock."

"Because it was so unexpected?"

"Because it obliterated his case. He certainly didn't expect it," Gordon replied.

"But it was the answer you expected, wasn't it?" Scott asked.

"I don't know what I expected. The witness was called by the prosecution. He was their witness. He couldn't identify the defendant. But it was a true answer—the answer that led to the acquittal," Gordon responded.

"It was what one could call the defining moment of the trial, wouldn't you say?" Scott asked.

"Turned out that way."

"Do you recall how you conducted your cross-examination?"

"My cross? A cross wasn't necessary. The witness failed to identify the defendant."

"And that's exactly my point, Mr. Gordon. You did in fact conduct a cross-exam, didn't you?"

"A very limited one," Gordon responded.

"And you began by having the defendant, your client, stand and face the witness, Josh Johnson, didn't you?"

"I believe I recall that."

Scott picked up a thick document from his table. It was marked, authenticated, and accepted into evidence as an exhibit.

"I have a transcript of that trial, Mr. Gordon. I'm going to read from it and ask if that's the cross-examination you conducted. The questions are yours, the answers by the witness, Josh Johnson.

"Question: *'Mr. Johnson, the man you saw with the pistol, did you have a profile view of him as you were looking through that window?'*

"Answer: *'Yes sir, I did.'*

"Question: *'A left profile or right profile?'*

"Answer: *'It was his left.'*

"Question: (to defendant) *'Mr. Harrison, turn so Mr. Johnson can see your left profile.'* (Defendant turned as directed). *'Is this the man you saw that night with the pistol?'*

"Answer: *'No, sir, it is not.'"*

Scott took a couple of steps closer to the witness. "Did I read that correctly, Mr. Gordon. Or would you like to see the transcript?"

"I don't need to see the transcript. That's about how it went."

"Now, Mr. Gordon, tell us—what experienced criminal defense attorney would have his client stand for *another* identification—this time a *profile* view—by a witness who had already, as you just said, *obliterated* the prosecution's case? What experienced criminal defense counsel would take such an unnecessary chance for the witness, who might finally say, 'Yes, that's the man'?"

"Well, it worked out fine."

"Yes, it worked out fine because you *knew* he would not make the identification. You bet $250,000 on it, didn't you?"

Gordon was again slow in answering, but Scott did not wait for an answer. "I have no further questions of this witness, Your Honor," Scott said, as he turned and walked to join Fasi at the prosecution table.

There was no redirect examination by Colosimo. Judge McCabe asked if the defense had any additional evidence.

"The defense rests," Colosimo replied.

"Does the prosecution have a case in rebuttal?" the judge asked.

"May we have a short recess, Your Honor—ten minutes?" Scott asked. He wanted to see if either of his missing witnesses had been located. He hoped he would be able to call at least one as a rebuttal witness. Judge McCabe granted the request, and Scott sent Bob McSweeney to check with Richard Evans on the progress in locating the witnesses.

McSweeney returned with the answer Scott expected—both were still missing. So, all the evidence was now in. His closing would be quite different than the one he had planned a couple of weeks ago, but he was confident he could convince the jury of the two charges of influencing witnesses, the only charges still before the jury. When the court reconvened, Scott announced he had no witnesses in rebuttal.

Judge McCabe looked at the clock on the courtroom wall. "We'll take an early lunch break now and reconvene at one-thirty. I want counsel to remain in the courtroom."

When the jury had departed, Colosimo renewed his motion for a directed verdict of acquittal to the remaining charges, which was quickly denied. Then the usual quibbling over jury instructions began. Despite the fact that the elements constituting the crime of influencing witnesses were clearly laid out in Section 16-10-93 of the Georgia Code, the spat did not end until almost 12:30 p.m. Scott had an hour to review what he would be saying in his closing argument. He had never tried a case that would end with a *mea culpa*—witnesses promised but not produced. He and Fasi discussed the best approach to the problem. They both concluded there was no easy way out. The only way to approach the dilemma was to admit the error and *be* sincere and *appear to be* sincere. This was made more difficult by the fact that Scott could not explain the reasons for their absence, even if he knew—which he didn't. The exhilaration he usually felt in preparing and making a closing argument was missing. This was going to be painful.

Chapter Thirty-Six

Wednesday, November 19

"Members of the jury," Scott began. "At the beginning of this trial, I stood before you—in this very same spot—and told you of two men who would testify that they had been paid to testify falsely at a criminal trial in September of last year. But, as the judge instructed you, the opening statement is not evidence. It's merely what we expect to present as evidence. And now you see the value of that instruction, because I was unable to bring those two men to this trial. As a consequence, Judge McCabe has dismissed the two charges that pertained to the expected testimony of these two witnesses. *Why* I was unable to present these witnesses is not something for you to consider in your deliberations. It simply is not an issue. It is not evidence, and those two charges are no longer before you."

Scott could feel a pain in the pit of his stomach. This was an opening no prosecutor should ever have to present to a jury. But he must, and he continued.

"What is before you *now*—what you must decide when you go back to the jury room to deliberate—is whether the defendant is guilty of the crime of influencing witnesses. And you must determine it from the facts that have been proved in this court.

"It is not my purpose to instruct you on the law of this case. That comes—must come—from Judge McCabe. But here are the questions you must answer in arriving at your verdict:

"Did a person give Vijay Patel or Josh Johnson some benefit, reward, or consideration?

"Was this benefit, reward, or consideration given with the intent to deter them from testifying truthfully in court?

"Was the person who did this the defendant in this case, Maxwell T. Gordon?" He turned and pointed directly at the defendant. "That man," he said.

"Members of the jury, you know the answer to each of these questions." He paused briefly before continuing. "But do you know the most *appalling* thing about all this?"

Scott stopped for a longer pause, turning his head slowly and making eye contact with each juror before answering his own question.

"It *worked!* John Harrison walked out of this courtroom a free man, thanks to those lies purchased with cash from the defendant." Scott expected an objection to this last comment. Because of the no-show of Patel and Johnson, he had presented no actual evidence that the false testimony ever occurred. But he believed it to be a fair argument considering the payment had been for that very purpose. In any case, Colosimo did not object.

He then went on to review the evidence provided by the testimony of Carl DeBickero and Clarence Wilborn. He displayed the enlarged photos of Patel and Johnson viewing their payments. He acknowledged the blemished character of Wilborn as well as the fact Wilborn was testifying with a pretrial agreement to reduce his own sentence. But he questioned what possible explanation there could be for the evidence—the uncontested evidence— that both Patel and Johnson received a suitcase filled with cash. *Who could have been behind such a plan? Who could have provided such a large amount of money? Who had the money, plan, and motive? Who but Gordon?* He was now ready to conclude.

"Members of the jury, the evidence is clear. As clear as the photos of Vijay Patel and Josh Johnson smiling as they looked at that $250,000, compliments of that defendant." Scott paused and pointed once again at Gordon.

"It is now your privilege, your duty, to render the judgment in this case. On behalf of the state of Georgia, I ask that you do nothing more than what you took an oath to do at the beginning of this trial—that you return a just verdict, a verdict that speaks the truth. A verdict that says this defendant is guilty of the two charges of influencing witnesses, as alleged in the indictment. And not because *I* say so, but because *the evidence* says so. Thank you for your service on this jury."

Colosimo did not wait for the judge to invite him to begin his closing argument. He was on his feet immediately.

"Isn't it convenient," he began, "for Mr. Marino to ask that you ignore the unfulfilled promises he made in his opening statement. To ignore the lies that Clarence Wilborn told you. To ignore the fact that the one person who appeared in this courtroom who had a compelling motive to lie was Clarence Wilborn. Do you recall his response when I asked him what benefit he was receiving for his testimony in this case? Instead of facing a possible sentence of life in prison, he will receive less than ten years, possibly much less. That, ladies and gentlemen, may be the only truth he told during the entire time he was in that witness chair."

And so it went, just as Scott had expected. A scorching excoriation of Wilborn's testimony and character, followed by the argument that the indictments resulted from the embarrassment of the district attorney in losing the case. And then a full report of the defendant's bio and professional accomplishments. As Grady had warned him months before, Colosimo, despite his garish dress and ostentatious display of diamonds and gold, was in fact, a formidable courtroom advocate. He had a powerful voice and a keen sense of drama. He had the rapt attention of each juror, and he missed nothing in pinpointing every weakness in the prosecution's case. When Colosimo was approaching the end of his argument, his voice became more modulated.

"Ladies and gentlemen of the jury. There is one part of the prosecutor's argument that we can agree with, and that is you have the duty to render a *just* verdict in this case. You took an oath to do so. You must hold the state to its burden of proof: beyond a reasonable doubt. *Believing* that Maxwell Gordon is guilty is not sufficient. Each and every one of you must believe in his guilt *beyond any reasonable doubt*.

"A verdict of guilty would be not only an unjust verdict affecting Maxwell Gordon for life, but a verdict that would affect all of you for the rest of your lives. Every day you will recall your service on this jury. Every day you will look back on this trial and ask yourself, 'Did I do the right thing? Did I do justice to that man? Wasn't there a serious conflict in the evidence? Wasn't there at least some reasonable doubt?' But then it will be too late. There will be nothing you can do to right that wrong. If you have any reasonable doubt, now is the time to say so. Tomorrow, next week, next year, will be too late. Do justice in this case *today*. Find Maxwell Gordon *not guilty*!"

Colosimo slowly turned his head from side to side, momentarily making eye contact with each juror, then walked to the defense table and took his seat.

Scott had made notes of each point that Colosimo had made. He tried to refute each one, but a rush of tension and three days of stress clouded his mind, and he felt physically weakened. At times he felt his hands shake, and trying to maintain eye contact with the jury as he checked his notes was difficult. With his vigorous voice dampened, and his body exhausted, he knew he must quickly conclude.

"I urge you to use your good old walking around common sense," he said, using what vocal strength he had left. "No one is required to leave common sense in the hallway when serving on a jury. Return the only verdict that is *just* and speaks the *truth*, a verdict of guilty to both charges."

He paused and took a step backward. Then he viewed the jury from side to side, trying to make eye contact with as many as he could. "Thank you," he said, as he returned to the prosecution table.

Scott knew his final closing was far from his best. The pressure of the trial had finally gotten to him. He could only hope that it was at least adequate to underscore the absurdity of the defense. He was unsure of how it was received, so the discrete handshake and smile from Fasi as he sat down at his table was comforting. He was at once relieved that this trial was over and disappointed in the way it ended—only two charges for the jury to consider. But he was satisfied that the jury had the necessary evidence to convict on both.

Judge McCabe ordered a twenty-minute recess, after which he would begin giving the jury instructions. The courtroom spectators began filing out, but Scott and Fasi remained at their table. They had only one remaining task, to listen carefully to the judge's instructions for any errors—this was not a trial they wanted to retry because of an instruction error. The room was almost cleared when they saw Luke Schaub approaching.

"I got a call a few minutes ago from a sheriff's deputy. Patel was picked up out at Tybee Island. He's now down at the county detention center."

"Well, isn't that dandy," Scott said. "The charges he was to help us with were dismissed six hours ago. So, he served himself up on a platter—goodbye pretrial agreement for a short sentence in the county jail. Hello, Vijay Patel, welcome to the state pen."

"The deputy who called me is the one who drove him from Tybee Island to the detention center. Apparently they had quite a talk on the way."

"About what?"

"About why he went missing."

"That should be interesting."

"It is. He said he showed up at the courthouse Tuesday morning, ready to testify and saw some guy by the name of 'Anderson.' Anderson was one of two men who visited him at his store a few weeks ago, giving him advice about a defense he had to the charge of perjury. The man with Anderson assured him he could beat the charge because of the 'two-witness rule.' Patel did some research with the help of a reference librarian at a public library. He believed it was true. And he wondered why his attorney—*that's me*—didn't tell him about it. The deputy asked him why he didn't tell me about it, and Patel said he was afraid because I had given him strict instructions not to discuss the case with anyone. He was confused but still planned to testify because he still trusted his attorney."

"But he didn't," added Scott.

"Right. Yesterday morning when he arrived at the courthouse, Anderson was standing near the entrance. Anderson said, 'Are you stupid?' That's all he said, but it made him rethink his options. He drove out to Tybee and just strolled the beaches, thinking. Didn't go home. They found him there this morning."

"Good deputy," Scott said. "Drew a lot of information from Patel during that thirty minute drive from the beach. He should be a detective. I think I know this guy 'Anderson.' Colosimo has an office goon with that name."

"You think Colosimo was involved in this?"

"Of course, fits his style. And it seems Patel gave an honest answer by leaving the courthouse to walk on the beach—yes, he's stupid."

"Sure seems that way," said Luke. "I had explained to him we could surely beat the perjury charge but not the conspiracy count. He was looking at five years, with a one year minimum. I made it clear that the pretrial was a total deal—plea to both and get a max of twelve months. It was a decent deal even at the twelve months, but it's entirely possible he would have served only a couple. But he blew it. I doubt he knows how bad he blew it."

"Maybe we'll offer him another deal—he may be able to avoid the state pen after all. We'll probably need his testimony against Colosimo and his gang of hoodlums."

"Good," Luke replied, as he noted the judge entering from the doorway near his bench. "I'll keep in touch," he added as he departed.

After Judge McCabe read the instructions to the jury, they retired to the jury room to deliberate. It was almost 4:00 p.m. The tense wait for the verdict now began.

Chapter Thirty-Seven

Wednesday, November 19

Scott and Fasi went to their offices to wait for the verdict. A bailiff would be stationed right outside the jury room to listen for the knock that the jury had a verdict. Then the clerk would call the attorneys to assemble in the courtroom. This was the phase of the trial that took the major toll on all participants, counsel as much as the defendant.

The Waiting. What a miserable, unbearable feeling, waiting for the verdict. Where could you go and what could you do, other than wait? It wasn't like waiting for a plane or train to arrive. Those were predictable, at least usually. Not so with a jury verdict. Some old salts say that a quick verdict means an acquittal. But what is a quick verdict? In 1971, the Charles Manson verdict took nine days. That's a long wait by most standards, but it might be considered a "quick verdict" when compared with the Thomas Maniscalco verdict in 1994. Maniscalco was a California biker-turned-lawyer-turned-killer who was found guilty of second-degree murder after the jury deliberated *twenty-four days*. Unbearable waiting.

The Waiting. Tom Petty and the Heartbreakers tell us, in their 1981 hit, "The Waiting," that "the waiting is the hardest part." The

Philadelphia Flyers played this song at the home games, when a play was being reviewed by the officials.

The Waiting. Lawyers like to be in control. Must be in control. But now it was entirely *out* of their control. Now the mind turned to the witness who was *not called*, the question that was *not asked*, the objection that was *not made*. Relentless second-guessing and self-reproach. It might be the attorney's first trial, or the hundredth, but the waiting was the same—a stressful, comfortless, utterly helpless feeling until you get that call—*the jury has a verdict.*

Scott had plenty of work on top of his desk, but no work would get attempted during "*the waiting*." He called Jennifer's cell.

"The jury's out," he said.

"Yes, I saw it on Channel 3. I was late getting to the courthouse and couldn't get a seat, so I went back to the Student Center to watch. There was a big crowd there. They were cheering your closing argument. Lot of interest here at the school. I thought you aced it, Scott. How do you feel?"

"Exhausted."

"I know, but I mean about the trial, the verdict."

"I don't know, Jen. We went into it with high hopes, solid case, then the witnesses performed their disappearing act. And the defense came up with the big lie. I've heard if you are going to lie, make it a big one—it works better on a jury. But it's preposterous. I can't believe the jury will buy into it, though I guess anything is possible when the key prosecution witness has no credibility—none. And Max Gordon is a celebrity, and as far as the jury knows, has an unblemished record. They don't know he's under investigation by every bar association he's a member of and even some he's not."

"Do you think you'll get a verdict today?"

"I sure hope so. Judge McCabe ordered food to be delivered at six. I'm sure he wants to finish today. I don't know how long he'll wait on a verdict before sending them home for the night."

"Well, I hope they bring in that verdict soon. I can tell you are pretty stressed."

"And I don't deny it," Scott replied.

"When you finish up there tonight, come on over, regardless of the time. I think I know how to relieve that stress."

Chapter Thirty-Eight

Thursday, November 20

Scott arrived at work the next day later than usual. No reason to get there before the jury, which would begin deliberating again at 9:00 a.m. At 10 p.m. Wednesday, Judge McCabe had questioned the jury foreperson about the progress they were making. She responded that they were indeed making progress but believed they were unlikely to reach a verdict soon. He dismissed the jury for the night with instructions to return in the morning to continue deliberations.

Scott sat at his desk, a stack of files in front of him, some old, some new, but none likely to get much attention that morning. His thoughts were of course on the trial. And the jury now deliberating. *What could be taking them so long? Surely they couldn't be buying into that cockamamie defense. It was ludicrous.* He thought of the lady who was now the foreperson. What was her background, her occupation? He reached for the yellow pad on which he made notes during jury selection. There—she was a CPA. *Surely she wouldn't be fooled by such an absurd defense.* But he recalled how attentive she was when Gordon was testifying. He felt a bit weak, then realized he had skipped breakfast. Jennifer usually made breakfast when he stayed over, but she was leaving for school just as he was waking up.

Fasi called him midmorning. "Am I interrupting anything special?"

"Hardly. Just sitting here staring at a stack of files, thinking about what that jury might be thinking."

"How about a cup of Starbucks from my magic coffee maker? Might as well wait here as there."

"Sounds great. I'm on the way." He left immediately for Fasi's office—a cup of coffee would perk him up.

They were comfortably seated, enjoying a fresh cup, when the phone rang. It was a bailiff. Judge McCabe wanted them in the courtroom ASAP. He didn't say why. It might be a verdict. Or it could just be a request from the jury for some testimony to be read or a question concerning the jury instructions. They put down their coffee and left immediately for the courtroom.

Unlike previous sessions, they found the courtroom essentially empty of spectators. The TV camera was still in place, an operator seated nearby reading a paperback. Scott was surprised to see both Colosimo and Gordon seated at the defense table. Apparently they had remained in the courtroom to await the verdict. The clerk and two bailiffs were present, but the judge and jury were absent.

Scott walked over to one of the bailiffs. "Do you know if it's a verdict, or just a question?" Scott asked.

"I wasn't the one who answered the knock, but I was told it's a verdict," he replied.

Scott and Fasi took seats at the prosecution table. Soon, a few members of the press began to drift in. Among them was Bill Baldwin. Scott was amazed at how quickly he got the word. That was typical Baldwin. He also recognized the two "associates" from Colosimo's law firm. They took seats directly behind the defense table. The last person Scott saw enter was Clarence Wilborn. He was wearing the same suit he wore when he testified, and it appeared that he had slept in it. Scott thought it strange that Wilborn was still hanging around. He would be sentenced soon for the crimes he had already pleaded guilty to, but he was still free on bail. Scott was sure that if he were in Wilborn's situation he wouldn't be wasting these last days of freedom sitting in a courtroom gallery.

The clerk picked up the courtroom phone and made a call. Shortly afterwards Judge McCabe entered and the bailiff ordered all in the courtroom to their feet with three loud raps on the floor with his tall staff.

"I've received word that we have a verdict," the judge said. "Bring the jury in."

Soon the jury was seated. The TV operator had put down his book and was standing ready behind his camera. The gallery was now about a quarter full. Several assistant district attorneys, and a couple of local attorneys who happened to be in the courthouse when the word of "a verdict in the Gordon case" went out, had also come in to observe. Judge McCabe turned to his right and looked toward the jury.

"Has the jury reached a verdict?"

The foreperson stood. "Yes, we have, Your Honor." She was holding the verdict form.

Suddenly—and surprisingly—Scott felt relieved, despite not knowing what the verdict was. It was just that the waiting was about over. The pressure that had remained since 4:00 p.m. the previous day was about to end.

"Please hand the verdict form to the bailiff."

The bailiff took the form from the foreperson and delivered it to Judge McCabe, who examined it carefully.

"The defendant and his counsel will please stand." The judge then handed the form to the clerk, who was seated down and in front of the bench. "Madam Clerk, publish the verdict."

Colosimo stood stiffly erect, with a tightened jaw, his gaze solidly fixed on the clerk. Gordon presented a look in contrast. He stood stooped and lifeless, his eyes unfocused and head bent forward, as if he had already heard the verdict and it was not good.

The clerk, a middle-aged African-American woman, stood, and with a strong voice began to read from the verdict form:

"State of Georgia versus Maxwell E. Gordon.

"We the jury in the above captioned case find as follows: As to Count One, Influencing Witnesses, Not Guilty. As to Count Two, Influencing Witnesses, Not Guilty. So say we all."

Chapter Thirty-Nine

Thursday, November 20

As soon as the verdict was read, Judge McCabe polled the jury, calling each member by name and asking the same question: "... is this your verdict?" After the twelfth affirmative "yes," he thanked the jury for their service, adjourned the court, and quickly left the bench.

Maxwell E. Gordon was a free man.

And with that, Gordon's stooped body came to life. He straightened up immediately, thanked and congratulated Colosimo with a smile and quick handshake, and walked to the bar rail. He was still smiling as he faced the media and spectators in the gallery.

"Could I have your attention?" he called in a loud voice. "I have something to say about this trial, and I'll be saying it outside in a few minutes, out by 'The Flame of Freedom.' All are welcome." He stopped and looked at the TV cameraman, who was standing behind his tripod and still recording. "Cameras also welcome!" Gordon then returned to the defense table, where Colosimo had remained during the short announcement.

Scott and Fasi had turned to watch Gordon as he spoke. They had not had time to reflect on the verdict. Now they faced each other, and both were at once speechless. Fasi extended his right hand to Scott and placed his left hand on Scott's right shoulder. He took a deep breath and slowly shook his head. Words did not come from either prosecutor.

"The Flame of Freedom" that Gordon referred to was a monument located in front of the Chatham County Courthouse, a few yards to the right upon exiting the courthouse. It was erected in 1969 as an "eternal flame of freedom," a tribute to veterans who offered their lives to preserve it. Gordon used the monument as a backdrop to a speech after the acquittal in the Harrison retrial.

"I don't think I'll be attending Max Gordon's little ceremony," said Scott.

"Good idea," Fasi responded. "Let's go up to my office and finish our cup of coffee."

"That's a much better idea," Scott replied as he watched the small crowd moving slowly toward the exit to the courtroom. One person in particular caught his eye. It was Clarence Wilborn, moving rapidly, pushing his way through the slower crowd.

Scott and Fasi took the elevator up to the sixth floor and Fasi's office. Fasi's Keurig machine quickly produced two cups of hot coffee, and the two were now seated in the same spots they were in when the bailiff called. They had not spoken since leaving the courtroom. Scott was still feeling the shock of hearing the words, "not guilty." He tried to erase the image in his mind of the smile on Max Gordon's face as the clerk finished reading the verdict. He was sure it would haunt him for a long time. He regretfully recalled that he had the opportunity to leave the case but chose not to. He recalled telling Juri, on the way back from their visit to Atlanta, that he "wanted to see the slimy bastard and his slimy client when the jury brings in the verdict." Well, he *had seen them*, and it wasn't a pleasing sight. Now he would just have to live with it.

The mood was somber, almost funereal, as the two sat in silence. Scott got up and walked over to a small table near Fasi's desk where there was a small television.

"Do you mind?" Scott said, pointing to the TV.

"No, I guess we should take a look at the celebration, since we played a leading role," Fasi responded.

Scott found the channel. It showed a crowd assembling in front of the memorial. Scott recognized several of the journalists who had been covering the trial. Bill Baldwin was among them. Gordon could be seen a few feet behind the memorial, but he was not speaking, perhaps waiting for the crowd to grow. The time was approaching 11:30 a.m., and the early lunch crowd was leaving the building. Many, seeing the tripod with the TV camera setup on the paved walkway facing the memorial, stopped to observe. Soon there was a crowd of a hundred or more.

Max Gordon stepped forward and faced the camera. He was all smiles.

"Thank you all for coming," he began. "How fitting it is that I'm able to make this speech in front of the 'Flame of Freedom.' This flame, which has burned so brightly for almost forty years, is a reminder of the precious heritage we—all Americans—enjoy. And that includes those of us accused of crimes we did not commit. I want to thank the good people of Savannah for making right this terrible wrong. And especially the members of the jury who saw through the lies told by the prosecution. And another special thanks to my defense team, led by one of America's foremost trial attorneys, 'Diamond Jim' Colosimo." He pointed to Colosimo, who acknowledged the accolade by extending both arms outward and upward, with middle and index fingers in a victory sign, reminiscent of Richard Nixon.

Scott continued to listen, anger building with every platitude uttered by his old nemesis. He turned to Fasi, who was staring at the screen with eyes narrowed and jaw clenched.

"I'm going to need a barf bag, Joe. This sounds like the same speech he made after he bought that acquittal in the Harrison case with his paid liars."

Before Fasi could respond, the screen revealed a man rushing toward Gordon. He had a pistol—a small automatic—in his right hand. As he reached Gordon, he grabbed the back of his shirt collar with his left hand and pulled Gordon backwards. The pistol immediately went up, making a hard contact with the back of Gordon's head. The man holding the pistol turned, facing the camera. It was Clarence Wilborn.

Chapter Forty

THURSDAY, NOVEMBER 20

"You're going to tell this crowd the truth," Wilborn shouted. "Now! Do it! Tell them the truth, you lying whore of an attorney. Now!" Wilborn, with a firm grip on Gordon's collar, twisted him so that he faced the camera. "Tell them how you used me, or your fucking head is going to explode." The crowd now began to disperse, some running toward the street, some ducking into the entrance to the courthouse. But the camera and its operator remained, along with a small crowd, apparently more curious than frightened.

Wilborn was less than six feet tall, thin and wiry, but obviously powerful. His one arm on Gordon was more than sufficient to control the rotund Gordon, even without the weapon that he held to back up his commands. Gordon's face was flushed, his eyes wide with fear, but his arms gave no fight to the man holding the pistol.

"Tell them how you—*you*—planned it and brought me in to help with the dirty work. Look at the camera! Tell them now, you filthy son-of-a-bitch!" Wilborn's pistol remained firmly against Gordon's head. He leaned into Gordon, shouting his commands into his left ear and tightening the hold on his collar. Gordon's eyes were bulging from their sockets.

"Turn me . . . loose . . . and . . . I'll . . . tell . . . them." Gordon was struggling to get the words out.

The event was being recorded live by the same cameraman Gordon had invited to his victory celebration. The commands by Wilborn were being heard clearly by Scott and Fasi as they watched the TV screen in Fasi's office. They glanced at each other frequently but said nothing. Scott looked carefully at the few remaining spectators for Colosimo, but apparently he was no longer present. Neither was Bill Baldwin. *Smart move on the part of both*, he thought, but he was sure that Baldwin had not wandered far and was observing from a safe distance. It would surely be his lead story the next day.

The camera suddenly turned from Wilborn and Gordon, and focused on a uniformed deputy who was slowly making his way through the remaining small crowd and moving toward Wilborn. But the deputy was spotted by Wilborn.

"Stay where you are," Wilborn shouted, "or I'll drill this fucker's head and then yours."

The deputy stopped and was heard to yell at the cameraman, "Turn the camera off. And everyone, out of here." All of the remaining spectators quickly fled, except two or three who apparently felt safe ducking behind the monument.

"Don't move that camera!" yelled Wilborn. "You move it, and I'll shoot this pervert between his ears. Keep that camera running. I want Savannah to know. This lying bastard paid two witnesses a quarter million each to fool a jury last year. Then used his own lies to fool a jury today. I'm to pay ten years for my crimes and he'll pay *nothing!* That's justice?" He jerked hard on Gordon's collar once more.

"Tell 'em, Max. Tell the truth. Who set up those payments? Who? Say it, Max!"

Sirens were heard on the TV. Scott quickly walked to Fasi's sixth floor window and looked out. He had a view of Montgomery Street and saw multiple vehicles heading toward the courthouse with blue lights flashing. The scene near the memorial was only partially visible from the window, so he turned back to the TV.

What Scott saw was the Metro Police SWAT and Hostage Negotiations Team going into action. They were surrounding the area, and Scott could hear the team commander calling for Wilborn to drop his weapon. Wilborn had maneuvered Gordon backwards toward the outer wall of the courthouse where there was some waist-high shrubbery. The picture of the scene was still being shown on the TV. The voices were indistinct, but at least two voices could be heard. One was Wilborn's. The camera showed him still holding his hostage in front of him by the collar, the pistol still firmly pressed into the back of his head. Wilborn now had his back flat against the building's outside wall.

The camera showed members of the SWAT Team inching closer from both the left and right. One held a scoped rifle in a kneeling position near the courthouse entrance. Then the audio became better, though not entirely distinct, as Wilborn began to shout his instructions to Gordon.

"You son-of-a-bitch, give me a good reason why I shouldn't blow your ass to hell right now!"

"You are right," Gordon was heard to say, in a loud but trembling voice. "I'm . . . I'm . . . sorry."

"Not good enough," Wilborn answered. "I'm going to count to five. You better have a better answer!"

Then Wilborn slightly loosened his grip on Gordon's collar and began to count slowly. "One . . . Two . . ."

"No! No!" Gordon wailed. "I'll make it right! I'll make it right."

"Three . . . I'm still listening!" Wilborn's voice was loud and demanding.

There was an eerie silence. The SWAT team stopped all movement.

"Four . . ."

Two shots rang out as the count reached five. One from Wilborn's pistol. The hollow-point projectile exploded in Gordon's head. The other shot was from the SWAT team member kneeling near the entrance. It caught Wilborn in the upper left side of his body, and he fell on his right side, into the shrubbery. His weapon flew out of his hand into the grass. He remained motionless as blood poured from his wound.

The response team of tactical paramedics went into action and the SWAT team commander began to secure the scene, directing the cameraman to leave. The TV coverage then moved to the studio, where newsmen recounted and replayed the events that had just occurred.

Scott and Fasi stayed in Fasi's office, glued to the TV, following the commentators as they discussed the scene they had just watched. The commentary soon became repetitive, but they continued to watch. It was announced that the medical examiner had found both Gordon and Wilborn dead when he arrived at the courthouse thirty minutes after the shooting.

After what must have been the fifth replay of the shooting, the phone rang on Scott's cell phone. It was Carl DeBickero.

"We just arrested Thomas Reid and Anderson McDowell," he said. "Got them before they could leave Savannah. Thought you would want to know."

"You bet. How about Colosimo?"

"Not yet, but he's next. The funds—the check that bought the Camaro in Birmingham—came from his law firm's operating account. We'll wait until we question his two assistants. I expect we'll have enough then to charge him. If not, I'm sure you can close the deal with a pretrial offer to one of the two we now have in custody."

"Good. Let me know what you need."

Just as they hung up, Fasi's desk phone rang. It was Janna O'Meara, the DA's secretary.

"Mr. Magidson would like to see you now, if it's convenient."

"It's always convenient when the boss wants to see me, " Fasi replied, with a laugh. "Is he aware of what just occurred in front of the courthouse?"

"Of course. I think that's what he wants to discuss with you."

"I'll be there in a minute."

Fasi turned to Scott, explained the phone call and quickly left. Scott returned to his office and called Jennifer.

When she heard his voice, she was relieved. "Oh, Scott. Are you all right? I just heard about the shooting."

"I was six stories up, watching on TV. I'm going to the Library. I think I need a beer, maybe two—and maybe Juri will pick up the tab for my first-hand account. Can you meet me there, say in about twenty minutes?"

"Sure. Twenty minutes. I'll be there. I love you."

The End.

Made in the USA
Middletown, DE
17 November 2015